Taking The Cake

A walk on the wild side with her favorite bad boy is just what this good girl needs!

Mollie Mason is sure her night can't get any worse. Stuck in an inflatable rubber cake, she overhears her fiancé slamming her to the entire guest list of his bachelor party—and then she catches him cheating! But discovering her high school crush has witnessed her humiliation is the icing on the cake.

Cade Gallagher has wanted Mollie for years. And when she asks him to help her prove to the world—and herself—that she's not just a good girl, he knows he'd be a fool to say no. But she wants a temporary fling. Will two weeks be enough time to convince her to take a chance on him—forever?

Warning, this title contains the following: explicit sex, graphic language.

Strip Tease

He's vice. She's nice. This potent mix has to be handled with care...

It seemed easy enough. Hit the local all-male strip club, pick a likely target, and hire him for her best friend's bachelorette party. But the stripper who catches Caroline's eye has a different agenda. He's an undercover cop, and Caroline ends up under arrest—for solicitation!

Tony DiMarco realizes too late that he's made a mistake. Caroline's reputation and business are suffering, and he feels responsible. He feels something else, too—the pull of red-hot desire. He wants Caroline, but she's afraid that he's just trying to make up for his mistake. Can this determined vice cop teach her to trust again?

Warning, this title contains the following: explicit sex, graphic language.

Challenging Carter

When the stakes are high, she's ready to shed more than her inhibitions—but will the man of her dreams rise to the challenge?

Dani's been in love with Carter forever. But she's nothing like the women he dates—glamorous, exciting, spotlight-ready. Instead, she's stuck in the "best friend" role and can't seem to find a way out of it. Until a scheduling mix-up finds her enrolled in a strip aerobics class. Now this buttoned-down wallflower is finding her wicked side—and liking it!

What in the world happened to Carter's best bud? She's gone from sweet to sexy in ten seconds flat—and Carter's lucky enough to be around for the ride of a lifetime. But he knows from past experience that relationships don't last. He's got to get things back on track before the most important friendship in his life is damaged forever.

Problem is, Dani has no intention of going back to being "just friends". It's about time someone challenged Carter's assumptions about love and friendship—and Dani's just the woman to do it!

Warning, this title contains the following: explicit sex, graphic language.

Tease Me, Please Me

Kate Davies

A SAMHAIN PUBLISHING, LTD. publication.

Samhain Publishing, Ltd.
512 Forest Lake Drive
Warner Robins, GA 31093
www.samhainpublishing.com

Tease Me, Please Me
Copyright © 2007 by Kate Davies
Print ISBN: 1-59998-630-2

Taking the Cake Digital ISBN: 1-59998-079-7
Strip Tease Digital ISBN: 1-59998-116-5
Challenging Carter Digital ISBN: 1-59998-324-9

Editing by Angie James
Cover by Scott Carpenter

This book is a work of fiction. The names, characters, places, and incidents are products of the writer's imagination or have been used fictitiously and are not to be construed as real. Any resemblance to persons, living or dead, actual events, locale or organizations is entirely coincidental.

All Rights Are Reserved. No part of this book may be used or reproduced in any manner whatsoever without written permission, except in the case of brief quotations embodied in critical articles and reviews.

First Taking the Cake electronic publication: August 2006
First Strip Tease electronic publication: October 2006
First Challenging Carter electronic publication: February 2007
First Samhain Publishing, Ltd. print publication: August 2007

Contents

Taking the Cake
~9~

Strip Tease
~93~

Challenging Carter
~175~

Acknowledgements

First, a big thank you to my amazing editor, Angie. You challenge me to improve my writing every step of the way, and I am so grateful for it.

To Rebecca Goings, who came up with the title for this anthology – you rock! Thanks for your creativity and wit.

And as always, to my wonderful husband. I love you.

Taking the Cake

Dedication

To David and the kids.

Thank you for living with dust bunnies, for tolerating the click-clack of the Alphasmart on every car trip, for eating yet another box of mac and cheese as I write late into the evening. Most of all, thanks for supporting me wholeheartedly as I pursue the dream of being a published writer. All my love.

Chapter One

If she never saw the inside of another cake, it would be too soon.

Mollie Mason shifted uncomfortably, hoping the music cueing her "arrival" would hurry up and start playing. The combination mask/headdress had shifted, leaving her able to see out of only one side, not that there was much to see at the moment besides the dark interior of a round rubber container. And to make matters worse, her spangly leotard was slowly creeping up her butt.

Of course, the pop-up rubber cake left little room to adjust either situation, so she was left crouching on all fours, legs cramping, a half-blind butt-flossing idiot.

At least it wasn't a real cake, she thought, blinking drops of sweat out of her eyes. She could be worrying about getting crumbs and frosting in unmentionable places.

Instead, she had plenty of time to wonder if it was possible to suffocate inside such a confined space.

"Seattle Tax Accountant Dies Inside Bachelor Party Cake." Yeah, that's the legacy she wanted to leave.

Still no music; if they didn't get her out of this thing soon she was going to completely freak out. And a sobbing, jabbering mess was probably the last thing anyone wanted to see tonight.

For a moment, she let herself wonder—very briefly—how Blaine was going to react when she popped out of the cake. Although the stripper she'd bribed to let her take over the cake-jumping job insisted this was the most modest outfit available, it still revealed far more than she was usually comfortable revealing. At least the mask would hide her identity from the other guys in attendance. She might want to surprise Blaine, maybe shock him out of the complacency that seemed to be creeping into their relationship, but she had no intention of letting his friends and co-workers know that the girl popping out of the cake tonight would be walking down the aisle next Saturday.

She might be feeling a little daring tonight, but she wasn't a complete moron.

Mollie stretched her neck from side to side, trying to work out the kinks that seemed to be multiplying with each second inside this cake-shaped casket. The weight of the headdress only added to her discomfort—how in the world did showgirls dance every night in Vegas wearing these things?

The scent of disinfectant spray and stale body odor wafted past her nose again, making her gag. How did the poor women who did this for a living tolerate it? Not that they had much choice—the strippers' union wasn't exactly a powerhouse in labor relations.

Showed what a sheltered life she led. Until tonight, she'd never even considered these issues.

Her hiding place lurched, nearly sending her sprawling on her butt. Mollie's heart rate accelerated. Someone was rolling the cake out into the middle of the hotel suite where the party was taking place. At least it would be over soon. Then she'd drag Blaine to a back room and let him in on the secret, plant a big kiss on him, and hightail it over to Caroline's place to collect her fifty bucks.

She'd fulfilled her terms of the dare, so Caroline had better not kick about paying up.

She'd be lucky if Mollie didn't insist on double for pain and suffering.

She shifted once again, trying to keep her legs from falling asleep, and settled back to listen for her cue.

ಸಾರ

Cade took a swig of his beer and tried to remember why, exactly, he was at this train wreck of a bachelor party. The music was big-hair-band crap, the beer generic kegger swill, and the conversational topics all ten years old.

It was his worst class-reunion nightmare, come to life.

But this was even worse than a class reunion. Because tonight was all about the man who was going to marry Mollie Mason.

Cade looked across the room and tried not to grimace. The happy bridegroom was extremely happy at the moment, thanks to an abundance of cheap alcohol and cheaper women. The strippers were taking turns draping themselves all over Blaine, and he was definitely not objecting.

Of all the guys in their graduating class, why in the world had she picked this loser?

He'd been stunned to hear that Mollie and Blaine were getting married. It had been one of the first bits of gossip he'd heard on his arrival back home after so many years away. The Golden Boy and the Ice Princess, Junior had laughingly called them. And then invited him to tag along to the bachelor party as well.

"It'll be just like old times," Junior had said, and Cade grudgingly agreed to go.

Not that he particularly wanted to relive the bad old days. But he'd hoped to find that Blaine had grown into the kind of man who deserved a woman like Mollie.

To his everlasting disgust, that hadn't occurred.

In fact, pretty much everyone seemed to be stuck in the same rut they'd occupied in high school. And they all assumed he was the person they knew back then, too.

The problem was, he'd changed. And the person he'd been back then was so far removed from who he was now, he could hardly recognize the guy everyone seemed to expect him to be.

Junior stumbled by and slapped him on the shoulder. "Glad you could make it," he slurred. As best man, Junior was in charge of the party, and it showed. The only classy thing about it was the hotel room where it was being held.

Cade checked his watch and wondered how soon he could sneak out without being too obvious about it. Now that he knew the depressing truth about Mollie's choice of husband, he really had no reason to stay.

He had no claim on her—he never had. They'd been nothing more than casual acquaintances, people who saw each other in the halls from time to time. She was always active and involved, while he circled the periphery of high school life. But she'd never looked down on him, never treated him like a second-class citizen.

He'd forgotten her high school nickname until Junior had mentioned it. Ice Princess. Sure, she'd been a bit reserved, almost shy. But never stuck up. He had the feeling most of the guys in this room had never bothered to look beyond the surface to see what she was really like.

Of course, he hadn't seen her in ten years. Maybe she'd become the kind of shallow, image-chasing female that Blaine had always hooked up with in high school.

Or the ones he appeared to be hooking up with tonight.

God, he hoped not. The thought that the one bright spot of his adolescent years had changed so much was enough to really depress him.

Across the room, Blaine was busy sticking his tongue down the throat of the nearest stripper. Cade took another drink, resisting the urge to roll his eyes. Here this guy was marrying the sweetest girl from their high school class a week from Saturday, and he was getting it on with skanks-r-us. There was even the obligatory "girl-popping-out-of-a-cake" routine coming up, if the sad-looking rubber cake being wheeled in from the other room was any indication.

Sad and pathetic.

Sort of like his life right now.

"So, Blaine, buddy! What's the old ball and chain up to tonight?" Junior waved his mug in the air, spilling brew across the hotel room floor.

Blaine removed his face from the cleavage of the woman currently giving him a lap dance and leered. "Doing my quarterlies," he said.

Raucous laughter boomed through the suite, drowning out the bump-and-grind music playing on the portable CD player the girls from Sunset Strip had brought with them. "Oh, my God," Junior crowed. "That sounds pretty kinky, even for you, Blainester."

Blaine didn't even look up, too busy groping the lap-dancer's ass. "Yeah, right. Give me a break. Mollie's so goddamn uptight she thinks doing it with the lights on is too kinky."

A chorus of groans met that statement, accompanied by lots of head-nodding. "She is pretty straight-laced," someone said.

Blaine snorted, pulling the stripper closer so they bumped together groin-to-groin. "Hell, talk about understatement. She's the poster child for repressed."

"Why the hell are you marrying her, then?"

Cade wondered the same thing. The bridegroom's attitude toward his bride-to-be sure left a lot to be desired. But considering the source, he wasn't particularly surprised.

The bigger question was, why the hell was *she* marrying *him*?

"She serves her purpose," Blaine said carelessly.

"What purpose?" someone yelled across the room. "If the sex isn't good, what else is there?"

Blaine shrugged, an interesting maneuver considering the stripper draped over him. "I never have to worry about my taxes."

"But do you really want to snuggle up to a copy of the tax code every night?" Junior shuddered. "Why take yourself off the market for something like that?"

Something like that? Cade glanced over at Blaine. There were now two strippers gyrating over him, shoving their surgically enhanced breasts right in his face.

"She's not bad looking," Blaine said, eyes never leaving the Silicone Hills and Valleys.

"Under all those layers," someone interrupted.

Blaine laughed. "She'll go a long way toward convincing my older clients that I'm settled, a family man they can trust."

The other guys hooted with laughter at that one. Cade was tempted to join them.

Blaine mock-glared at them. "Hey, it's a possibility. You know that in my job, image is everything. Mollie fits that image. Plus, she's so busy with her own career I don't have to worry about her paying attention to my extracurricular activities." He leered at the brunette on his right knee, flipping open her bikini-style top so he could have easier access. She just grinned and leaned forward.

Cade could almost see the dollar signs spinning in her eyes. The ladies of Sunset Strip were anticipating some mondo-huge-o tips tonight. Enough to relax the rules against fraternization.

They were in for a major disappointment. Cade may have been away from this crowd for years, but he knew the type. The girls would be leaving with the bare minimum tip-wise. He almost—*almost*—felt sorry for them.

"So what you're telling me," Junior said, blinking owlishly, "is that you're marrying Mollie for her respek—respetik—"

"Respectability," Cade ground out, unwilling to listen to another drunken attempt. He had his limits.

"Yeah. What he said," Junior said. "She's 'spectable, and not bad looking, and won't have a clue that you're cheating on her."

"In a nutshell, my friend," Blaine gasped. Probably because the redhead on his left knee was busy undoing his pants.

Couldn't the asshole get a room or something?

Cade moved toward the door, setting his half-empty mug on the nearest table. Then someone punched a button on the

CD player and a classic strip tune started blaring through the tinny speakers. The partiers crowded around the rubber cake, blocking Cade's escape route.

He sighed inwardly, throwing a few curses at the god of bad timing, and crossed his arms. One girl popping out of a cake, and he was out of there.

The music swelled, filling the room with cheesy bump-and-grind notes. The fake cake shook a little, rocking from side to side as the girl inside apparently tried to get out.

Cade checked his watch, wondering just how long she was going to drag this out.

Finally, the hinged top of the cake flew open. The stripper rose out of the opening, looking more than a little shaky. The mask covering her face was tilted at a crazy angle, and she reached up and wrenched it around so it was in the right place.

She didn't have the typical "hi boys, aren't you glad to see me" look. In fact, her fists were clenched at her sides, her shoulders thrown back. She was radiating fury. Her gaze was riveted on the guest of honor.

Cade looked over at Blaine, frowning. He was oblivious to the attention, currently busy with the Titty Twins. One was holding his head to her ample breast, while the other was leaning over his unbuttoned pants, bobbing her head up and down enthusiastically.

The newest stripper stomped her way out of the cake, pulling down the backside of her outfit as she went. Ripping the mask off, she flung it at Blaine. "You pig," she hissed, and stormed out of the room.

Chapter Two

Oh, God. He knew that face.

Cade looked around at the other partiers, wondering which one would be the first to comment. To his amazement, none of the guys looked shocked. In fact, the majority seemed more confused than anything.

"What was up *her* butt?" Junior picked up the headdress, which had bounced harmlessly off Blaine's shins and dropped to the floor. As a grand gesture, it had failed miserably. The jerk hadn't even noticed.

The other partygoers crowded around Junior, inspecting the headdress and offering theories about the reason behind the stripper's tizzy fit.

Not one suggested it was because that stripper was the guest of honor's fiancée.

What in the world had Mollie been doing in that cake, dressed like that? Sure, in the world of Sunset Strip, the outfit was practically Amish, but Mollie Mason in a sequined leotard was an image he wasn't likely to forget anytime soon.

Cut low in front and high on the thigh, it had highlighted a lush body he'd never suspected was hiding behind those conservative outfits she wore. He'd fantasized, yeah, but never known for sure. Her breasts were high and full, curving enticingly at the low neckline. Obviously natural, too, a bonus after seeing enough implants this evening to start a factory. He could just imagine cupping them in his hands, brushing his thumbs across her nipples and watching them tighten in response.

Her behind was curvy, too, and she probably considered it the bane of her existence, but Cade closed his eyes briefly at the thought of gripping that sweet ass as he slowly thrust into her.

Over and over and over again.

Forget the fact that she'd tossed the headpiece and revealed her face. How could Blaine not know it was Mollie by her body?

Cade had only seen it once, and he knew that he'd never forget it.

Shaking his head once again at the blindness of the people surrounding him, Cade slipped out of the room. It wasn't likely he'd even be missed.

ᏕᏫᏣ

Oh God. Oh God oh God oh God. Mollie leaned over, bracing her hands on her knees. She counted her breaths, in for four, out for eight, trying not to hyperventilate. Passing out in the stairwell would just be the perfect ending for a perfectly hideous evening.

It was bad enough listening to Blaine slam her to all of his friends. She'd sat in that stupid cake, horrified, as he called her frigid. Oblivious. Easy to cheat on. A business asset, for God's sake.

A sexless lap dog he could trot out for company.

Then, when she was good and mad, she'd finally gotten out of that hellhole disguised as a cake to discover him cheating on her right in front of her face!

Not that he had any idea that the stripper jumping out of the cake was his fiancée, but the principle was the same.

Mollie closed her eyes, willing the image away. It was so sleazy, so—disgusting, to know he took their impending vows so lightly.

Lightly? They were nothing but an inconvenience to him.

Just like she was.

No. She was not going to cry, dammit. The slimeball didn't deserve it. He hadn't even bothered to react to her appearance, hadn't even *noticed* that she was in the stupid room, and certainly wasn't trying to track her down to apologize.

Of course, what would he say? "Sorry, honey, I have no idea how my dick ended up in her mouth."

Mollie straightened up, brushing the tracks of tears off her cheeks. She refused to leave any sign of weakness, hated that she was crying over that pitiful excuse for a man, but sometimes emotions couldn't be helped.

Though come to think of it, the primary emotion she felt right now was rage. She was furious at how he'd described her, fuming mad at the disgusting antics he had been engaged in when she finally escaped her bachelor-party prison. But she wasn't sad or grieving.

Shouldn't she be? After all, tonight had spelled the death of their relationship.

Maybe that would come later. What were the five stages of dealing with a lying, cheating, conniving ex-fiancé?

Ex. Oh, man. The wedding was in a week. How in the world was she going to cancel everything in one stupid week?

Because there was no way in hell she was going to go through with the wedding now.

She pushed up from the concrete step and straightened her outfit, wishing she could get her real clothes before heading home. But they were stuck in the bathroom of the hotel suite, and she wouldn't go back in that room on a bet.

Which was what had gotten her into this mess in the first place.

Caroline was going to pay.

Swearing under her breath, Mollie reached for her purse, then swore again as her hand swept through empty air. Of course her purse was still in the hotel suite. No self-respecting stripper would pop out of a cake carrying her Dooney and Bourke. And she was nothing if not self-respecting.

She leaned against the door, dropping her head back with a satisfying clang that echoed through the stairwell. She was going to have to go back in that damn room—because without her purse, keys, and cell phone, there was no way to get home.

Groaning, she banged the door again—then yelped as it opened behind her, sending her tumbling out into the open hallway and onto the carpet.

Right in front of a pair of black leather motorcycle boots.

"Thought I'd find you here," a very low, very familiar voice said.

Oh, no. No no no... Wincing, Mollie slowly raised her eyes, skimming up a pair of well-worn, well-fitting jeans, past a chambray button-down shirt, all the way up to a face out of a thousand fantasies.

And tonight, one hideous nightmare.

Face flaming, she scrambled to her feet, crossing her arms over her chest in a futile effort to hide her pseudo-outfit. "Cade," she mumbled, looking down at the ground. Of all the people who could possibly find her like this, why did it have to be him? "What are you doing here?"

"Hey, Mollie," he said, as if he saw her wearing a spangled bathing suit every day. "Thought you might need these."

His hand thrust into her field of vision, holding her neatly folded clothes and, thank heaven above, her purse.

"I—uh—thanks." She grabbed her things out of his hand. "How did you know..."

This time, she looked at him in time to catch a negligent shrug. "I asked one of the other girls where they had changed, and grabbed your stuff on the way out. Figured you wouldn't be in the mood to go back in."

She grimaced. "Not in a million years." Still utterly self-conscious of how little she was wearing, Mollie pulled on her sweatshirt right over the showgirl outfit. The girl she'd borrowed it from would just have to wait to get it back.

Or maybe she'd just burn it and send some money for a replacement.

"So, are you, um," Mollie waved her hand in a vague gesture, "did anyone say..."

"No one else recognized you." Cade glanced over his shoulder at the hotel suite. Loud music and raucous laughter pulsated through the closed doorway.

"I'm not sure if I should be relieved or insulted." She hiked her jeans up over her sequined butt. After a few failed attempts, she finally managed to secure the button. "Not even Blaine?"

"Sorry." Cade reached down and snagged her panties off the carpet where she'd dropped them in her haste to get dressed.

Mollie snatched them out of his hand and stuffed them into her pocket, along with her bra, which was draped across the toe of her spike-heeled shoe. "Okay, my humiliation is complete. Could you go now?"

"If that's what you—" He turned around abruptly, grabbed her by the shoulders and thrust her to the wall. Threading his fingers through her hair, he stepped into the vee of her legs and pressed her up against the wall with his body.

Dimly, she was aware of the sound of a door slamming, quickly swallowed up by the sensation of Cade's delicious body pressed against her from knee to chest.

God, he was built, with pecs that brushed against her breasts, causing her nipples to tighten almost painfully. His thighs held her legs apart, keeping her upright, which was a good thing since otherwise she suspected she would be a whimpering puddle at his feet. His fingertips traced tiny circles on her scalp, sending a tingle down to her toes.

He tilted her head just a little to the left, then crushed his mouth against hers, sweeping his tongue inside on her gasp of surprise.

And then it didn't matter that her rat of a fiancé had just betrayed and belittled her to all of his pals, or that her dream of a perfect marriage had crumbled into ash, because Cade was kissing her with all the heat and passion and finesse that she'd dreamed of since adolescence. Heat spiraled through her and she wrapped her arms around his neck, pulling him even closer, until the hard ridge of his arousal nudged her belly.

Oh, my God. Cade wanted her. She tilted her hips inward, rocking against him in a rhythmic motion that echoed the dance of his tongue stroking hers. Lifting one leg, she wrapped it around his waist and pressed against his rock-solid hard-on.

He growled into her mouth and slid his hands down to cup her buttocks, urging her other leg up to join the first until she wrapped completely around him, sex to sex, heat to heat. He gripped her tightly with one hand, the other sliding underneath her sweatshirt to cup her breast, teasing and tantalizing her aching nipple through the thin fabric of the leotard. It beaded even tighter under his ministrations, and she tangled her fingers in his hair, pouring years of desire into the kiss.

Suddenly, he pulled away, breathing erratically, his forehead pressed against hers. "I think they're gone," he whispered harshly.

Gone? Mollie looked over his shoulder at the empty hall. The elevator at the far end slid shut with a click.

"Sorry about that." Cade eased her down to a standing position. "It was all I could think of."

All he could think of? The best, most intense, most— arousing kiss of her entire life, and he was telling her it was just a fake?

Mollie stumbled a few steps away, clenching her hands at her sides to control the trembling. Or maybe to keep herself from touching him again. Of course the kiss was a fake. Just like the cake she'd jumped out of. Just like the engagement she'd thought was the real thing.

But nothing about her now-dead relationship with Blaine had ever come close to the passion she'd felt in one all-too-brief encounter with Cade Gallagher.

"I've got to get out of here." She hitched her purse onto her shoulder and pushed the stairway door open.

"Sounds good to me." Cade reached out and held the door for her.

She looked back at him in surprise. "You're coming?" Then blushed as a wicked grin spread across his face. "I mean, don't you want to go back to the party?"

"Are you kidding?" He followed her into the stairwell. "Let's hit the road."

※

Mollie Mason drove a mint green Volkswagen Beetle. Cade folded himself into the passenger seat, a little surprised at the whimsy of her vehicle choice. He'd have expected something more on the lines of a Camry or an Accord, a practical sedan with good resale value.

Instead, she drove a hippie-chick Bug—something flirty and girlie.

It just didn't compute.

Of course, he'd never expected Mollie Mason to drop her panties at his feet, either.

Even now, he had to shift in his seat to hide the evidence of his reaction. Just thinking about her made him hard, let alone sitting so close to her in a vehicle obviously not designed for the male of the species.

He gave a fleeting thought to his Harley, still parked in the underground lot at the hotel. He'd have to pick it up later. But the minute Mollie offered to give him a lift, he knew there was no way he would pass up that opportunity. No matter how uncomfortable the seating arrangements.

"There's a lever under the seat if you need to move back a little. Right between your—" She waved in the general vicinity of his knees, her face flushing a bright red. Pressing her lips together, she eased the car out of the parking space, once again avoiding eye contact.

Well, okay. He shifted his seat to the farthest-back position, letting out a sigh of relief as his knees vacated the area near his kidneys. "Definitely a girl car," he commented, stretching out the kinks.

She shot him a glare. "That's a sexist remark. Lots of guys like the new Beetle."

He held up a hand. "I didn't say I didn't like it. It's just not a great fit."

She glanced over at him, then looked back at the road. "I see your point." A smile flirted at the corner of her mouth.

Well, yeah. Hard to argue that a six-foot-three former Marine would be comfortable in here.

In her bed, well, that would be a different story.

His fingers itched with the need to touch her again. If the chime of the elevator hadn't reminded him they were in a public hallway, he would have found a way—any way—to get under those layers to the luscious body he now knew was hidden beneath.

God help him, he wanted her naked. Now.

"Can I ask you something?"

Cade shook himself. Now was not the time to be daydreaming about sex with Mollie. "Okay," he said slowly.

"Why in the world were you at the party? You don't even live in Seattle anymore, and I didn't think you and Blaine were friends."

He'd asked himself the same question a dozen times this evening, and still couldn't come up with a valid answer. Clearing his throat, he said, "I ran into Junior a few days ago at the airport, and he invited me to drop by. Thought it might be interesting to see some of the old gang."

Mostly, he'd been curious about Mollie's choice of husband material. He hadn't been impressed. Luckily for him, by the end of the evening, neither had she.

"Are you in town on business?"

"Personal business. I'm clearing up my dad's estate." He'd also been toying with the idea of moving back to town, but nobody knew that yet. Most likely, nobody would care. It wasn't as if he'd put a lot of effort into maintaining friendships since he'd left Seattle. For the past decade he'd been pretty footloose, traveling around the country and beyond, living out of a suitcase. Now he thought he might actually be ready to put down some roots.

"Couple of weeks in town, then." She glanced in the rearview mirror. "Where do you go from here?"

"Dallas," he said, which was true; he had a short-term contract with a company there.

Mollie sighed, her sweatshirt-covered breasts rising briefly into his line of sight. "You lead such an exciting life," she said, a wistful note in her voice.

"It's not that thrilling." He shifted in his seat. "Lots of hotel rooms, lots of takeout food."

"I've hardly been out of Seattle since we graduated. I was really looking forward to Hawaii."

"When are you going to..." Oops. Open mouth, insert foot. To the ankle. "Sorry."

"Don't be." She flashed him a wobbly smile. "Maybe I can go without him."

"You should." *Maybe I should go with you.*

No, dangerous train of thought. Time to change the subject. And maybe find out the answer to the question bugging him since she emerged from that cake like an avenging angel. "So, now you know what I was doing at the bachelor party from hell. What's your excuse?"

He studied her out of the corner of his eye. Other than a tightening of her fingers on the steering wheel, there was no reaction.

"Let's call it temporary insanity and leave it at that," she suggested.

He looked at her and raised one eyebrow. She sighed and began to talk.

Bingo. Worked every time.

"My girlfriend dared me to do it. I thought it would be a fun prank, something Bla—something he and I could laugh about later." She shook her head. "Don't see that happening now."

"Weren't you worried someone would recognize you?"

"Someone did." She raised an eyebrow back at him. "What I want to know is, why you and no one else? I mean, you haven't seen me in a decade, and I see the other guys all the time."

Good question. And not one he wanted to give an honest answer to. No way was he admitting he knew far more about her, going all the way back to high school, than a one-time casual acquaintance had a right to know. "You tossed your headdress thingy at him," he said. "I saw your face."

"So did every other guy in that room, and none of them figured it out."

Damn, she was quick. Okay, try again. "Your reaction," he blurted out finally, latching onto the most plausible explanation. "Anyone who would call the guest of honor a pig and stalk out had to have a personal stake in things."

She nodded, lips tightening. Not for the first time, Cade cursed Blaine for causing this sweet woman so much pain. Then sent up a prayer of thanksgiving that he was around to help pick up the pieces.

Maybe he was an opportunist. Hell, probably. But he'd wanted Mollie Mason for years now, and damned if he was going to be sorry her engagement had ended.

∞◊∞

"More coffee?"

Mollie shook her head at the waitress, covering her mug for emphasis. Any more caffeine and she'd start jitterbugging across the vinyl seat.

Oh, who was she kidding? If her nerves were on edge, it had far more to do with the man sitting across from her than the coffee in her system.

She pulled another napkin out of the metal holder, replacing the one she had systematically turned to confetti as she and Cade had talked. Their conversation had been easy and superficial—what they'd been doing since graduation eleven years ago, favorite movies, the upcoming election—but the underlying sexual tension had her more on edge than she could ever remember.

Hence, the napkin-shredding. She looked down at the blizzard of paper on the Formica tabletop and grimaced.

"You okay?" Cade's eyes were warm and concerned, looking right at her in a way she couldn't remember ever having experienced before. Even Blaine had only listened to her with half his attention, the rest focused on who was in the vicinity, people he could schmooze, and his next deal.

How pathetic was it that she'd never noticed that before tonight?

"I'm fine," she said, tossing her hair back in an approximation of bravado. "Never better."

He just looked at her steadily, not saying anything, his chocolate eyes unwavering.

She glanced away. "Humiliated. Angry. Numb."

"Brokenhearted?"

Mollie looked up at that. Was he watching her a little more closely for the answer? "Not particularly. I think I've known for a while things were bad. Maybe not this bad, but bad enough." She traced a circle in the puddle left by her glass of ice water. "At least I found out before the wedding."

Cade nodded, still giving her time and space to work out what she wanted to say. God, the luxury of being able to finish her own thoughts without being interrupted or corrected.

"I need your help, Cade." The statement clearly surprised him almost as much as it surprised herself.

"Anything." He reached over and covered her hand with his. "Whatever you need."

"I need—" She swallowed past the sudden dryness of her throat. Was she really going to go through with this? "I need you, Cade."

He stilled, his hand tightening on hers for a moment. "What exactly are you asking, Mollie?" His voice was low and rough, and a shiver of anticipation thrilled down her spine.

"I think you know." Did she have to spell it out for him? This was difficult enough as it was.

His other hand reached over and grasped her chin gently, lifting her head so that their eyes met. "Why?"

"Uh..." *Oh, smooth, Mollie. Way to impress him with your winning arguments.*

"Mind you, I'm not saying no," he continued, still holding her gaze. "I just need more information."

Mollie nodded. Best to have all the facts on the table before making a decision. "Blaine said some horrible things about me tonight, Cade. I want to prove that they're not true."

"I see."

Did he really? She rushed on, before she could lose her nerve. "He said I was boring and frigid and clueless. And the other guys there agreed with him."

"Those idiots?" Cade grimaced. "Hell, Mollie, they'd agree that the sun was purple if it meant free beer."

"I know." Mollie leaned forward. "But it still kills me that I've got that reputation. There's more to me than my job, you know. I'm an interesting person."

"I know you are."

"More than that, I'm a woman."

"I know that, too." His gaze dropped, slowly studying what he could see of her over the table. Her thighs flamed at the heated approval she could read in his eyes.

"I want to prove him wrong, Cade," she said hoarsely. "Will you help me?"

A flash of something close to disappointment surfaced in his eyes, but disappeared before she could focus on it. "I see."

"I'm not the woman he described," she said, trying to erase the look in his eyes. "But I'm also not as uninhibited as I'd like to be."

"And you think I'd be the right person to help you explore that side." A frown creased the space between his brows.

"Well, think about it." She waved a hand at him. "You live on the wild side—you always have. I don't mean that in a bad way, just that you never put too much stock in convention or rules. Who better to help me break a few rules of my own? Plus, you're just in town temporarily, so we won't have to worry about any awkwardness. You know, afterwards."

He was quiet for a minute, lips narrowed. "I don't know, Mol…"

"Please." She gripped his hand with both of hers, shocked at how badly she wanted him to agree. "I can't do this on my own."

He sighed, frustration oozing out of every pore. "It's a nice idea, but…"

"Never mind." She dropped her half-shredded napkin on the table. "If you aren't interested, Cade, all you have to do is say so. I'm sure someone else would be happy to help me explore my wicked side. Maybe Junior, or, or…"

Whatever other name she was trying to dredge up was driven completely out of her head as Cade leaned across the table and planted a big, deep, thorough kiss on her. His tongue stroked into her mouth, setting nerve endings ablaze. Too soon, the kiss ended, Cade sliding back into his seat. He leaned toward her, elbows on the table, a hot possessiveness visible in his eyes that sent a shiver down Mollie's spine.

"No one else, Mollie," he said, his low voice a promise. "No one teaches you. No one touches you. Only me."

"'Kay." She resisted the urge to touch her lips to see if they were as swollen and hot as they felt.

"But we do it my way," he said, laser-beam gaze still focused completely on her.

"Uh…"

"Good." He nodded as if she'd given full agreement. "We'll start with going to bed."

Her eyes widened. "Bed?" she squeaked, trying to ignore the tingle of desire centering between her legs.

A slow smile spread across his face, lighting his eyes with a devilish spark. "Separately."

"Oh."

He grinned. "It's been a long day and a longer night, and you need your rest."

Face flaming, she nodded. Privately, she wondered if she'd ever get to sleep, especially with memories of Cade's kisses to keep her awake. Not to mention the promise of tomorrow.

He rose, tossing a few bills on the tabletop. Holding out a hand to her, he pulled her to her feet. "Tomorrow," he said, as if he could read her mind.

Or maybe, she hoped desperately, he was looking forward to it as much as she was.

ಎಂಡ್

Cade yanked off his boot and flung it across the bedroom. It hit the wall with a satisfying thunk, so he did the same with the second one.

Nope, still felt as crappy as he had before he started.

What the hell was wrong with him? He should be ecstatic. He'd just been propositioned by the one woman he'd wanted since high school.

And that was the problem. Like everyone else, she still saw him as the guy he was back then. The bad boy, the slacker with the dangerous attitude. Rebel without a clue, he thought with a snort.

He wasn't that kid anymore, hadn't been for years. He wanted Mollie to want him for who he was, not for who he used to be.

If that was all Mollie wanted, though, he'd take what he could get.

He stripped off his shirt, tossing it on the chair next to the bed, then shucked his jeans and boxers and strode naked into the adjoining bathroom.

Even a cold shower did nothing to calm his raging erection. Toweling off, he grimaced at his reflection in the mirror. He'd already agreed to Mollie's suggestion. So why wasn't he slaking his desire in her bed, rather than suffering alone?

With his miserable luck, she'd come to her senses overnight and cancel the whole thing in the morning.

His fists clenched at his sides as he thought of losing this opportunity to show Mollie she was none of those things Blaine had accused her of being. Losing the chance to make love to her. Hell, she should be under him right now.

Or on top. Where Mollie was concerned, he wasn't choosy.

But he'd gone home alone tonight anyway. He might be selling his soul for a chance to fulfill the fantasies he'd carried around for so long, but he wasn't willing to take the chance that she'd wake up with regrets.

No, he'd suffer this long, aching night alone. But tomorrow morning he'd find out if Mollie still wanted him to be her guide for all things wicked.

Cade stretched out on the bed, tucking his hands behind his head. A slow smile curved his mouth. No, she wouldn't back down. He wanted Mollie Mason, and he always got what he wanted. After tonight, he wouldn't be sleeping alone.

୨୦୯୧

The phone rang six times before Caroline picked up. "H'lo?"

35

"It's me."

"Oh!" There was a fumbling sound, then Caroline's voice got clearer. "So how did it go?"

Mollie gripped the receiver and grimaced. "Hell would have been preferable."

"Oh, honey." Her best friend's voice softened. "Are you okay?"

Mollie swallowed. "Yeah, I think I am. But I need to ask you a favor."

"Anything."

"I need you to cancel all the wedding plans for me." She winced and held the receiver away from her ear as Caroline's screech threatened to pierce her eardrums.

"You're canceling the wedding?"

"Yeah."

"What happened?"

Mollie sighed. "Let's just say the creep was more interested in the strippers—plural—in his lap than the one jumping out of the cake."

"He *wasn't!*"

"Oh, yes, he was."

"And you actually saw them?"

"In the flesh. Literally."

"I never liked the asshole anyway. I only agreed to be maid of honor because I adore you. I can't say I'm sorry the wedding's off."

"Me, either." And to her surprise, it was true. It felt like a huge weight had been lifted off of her, leaving her almost buoyant. Yet another sign that marrying Blaine would have been a huge, monstrous, life-destroying mistake.

A strange rustling sound drew Mollie's attention. "Caro, what are you doing?"

Her best friend's voice was muffled. "Getting dressed. You shouldn't be alone."

"No!" Mollie jumped up. "You don't have to do that. It's late, and..."

"That's what friends are for," Caroline said. "Or if you'd rather, I could stop by tomorrow morning and we can take care of the cancellations together."

"I can't." Mollie swallowed. "I, uh, have plans."

"Plans?" Caroline's voice sharpened. "What kind of plans?"

"Well, I—" Mollie shrugged, even though Caroline couldn't see her. "I sort of ran into an old friend and we're going to get together tomorrow."

"Oh, good. At least you won't be alone."

Mollie's thighs clenched at the thought of how not alone she was going to be.

With Cade.

"So do I know her?"

She rolled her eyes heavenward. There was no way she was getting out of this conversation unscathed. "She's a he, and I'd rather not say."

That was the problem with long-time friends. They knew too many long-time secrets.

If Caroline knew that the mystery man was Cade Gallagher, Mollie would never hear the end of it.

Much as she wanted to spill all the gory details, she wanted to hold this experience to herself, just for a little while.

There was a long pause. "Girl, I don't even know you anymore."

"It's not like that," she lied, crossing her fingers.

"It's exactly like that," Caroline said with a knowing laugh. "And I think it's great. I'll just expect all the details later."

"Sorry I woke you."

"I'm not," Caroline replied. "Best news I've had in ages. Now don't worry. I'll take care of everything, and you have a good time."

"You bet." After promising to keep her informed, Mollie hung up the phone and stared blindly in front of her. In less than ten hours, she'd be with Cade again. He'd agreed to be her tutor in all things wild, which alternately thrilled and terrified her. She'd be living out a fantasy she'd carried with her for years, since high school, one she'd assumed could never come true. But now...

Oh, my God.

There was not a chance she'd get any sleep at all tonight.

And if she was lucky, there wouldn't be much sleeping going on tomorrow night either.

Maybe it was only for a limited time, but she was determined to get as much pleasure out of the experience that she possibly could. Because once Cade moved on, all she'd have left were the memories.

Hopefully, that would be enough.

Chapter Three

The doorbell rang promptly at nine a.m.

Mollie dropped her purse, her fingers clumsy with nerves. Fumbling with the straps, she walked down the hall to the front door.

Oh, God. What was she getting herself into?

The bell buzzed again, sending her heart rate into dangerous territory. This was a mistake. She didn't really mean what she'd said last night. All she had to do was open the door, explain everything to Cade, and forget she'd ever propositioned him last night.

Momentarily bolstered, Mollie pasted a smile on her face, swung open the door—

And blinked, twice, as her tongue sealed itself to the roof of her mouth.

He was lounging against the porch support, arms crossed casually over his chest. Clad in tight, tight jeans, a snug white T-shirt, and black leather jacket, he was every teenage fantasy come to life.

On someone else, it would have looked affected, a costume meant to make a point. But not on Cade. He was born for that look.

Everything about him, from posture to expression to attitude, looked relaxed and casual. But beneath the surface, Mollie could see a fine tension to him, a powerful energy that reminded her of a sleek jungle cat, eyeing its prey.

She swallowed, mouth dry as dust. "I have a list," she blurted out.

He raised one eyebrow. "Good morning to you, too," he said.

She was a class-A idiot. "Morning," she mumbled.

Cade reached out and snagged her hand, lacing his fingers through hers in a move that took her breath away. "Ready?"

No. Yes. Mollie shook her head, panic rising. "Uh, Cade..." she began.

He tugged her forward, still holding her hand in his. She stumbled a few steps until they were standing toe-to-toe, mere inches apart. "Let's try this again," he murmured, mouth so close his breath whispered through her hair. "Good morning, Mollie." He lowered his mouth to hers.

Unlike the incendiary quality of their earlier kisses, this one was slow. Smooth. He teased the seam of her lips with his tongue, encouraging her to open to him.

Desire slammed into her, so hard and fast she felt dizzy with it. Opening her mouth, she caressed his tongue with hers, reveling in the groan that sounded in the back of his throat.

His hand stroked down her back, curving over her behind to pull her hips in tight. The thick ridge of his erection nudged her waist, and she moaned, kissing him even deeper.

Slowly, he pulled back, nipping at her lips, her jaw, her throat. She drew in a ragged breath, her head tilted back, her eyes closed. "Wow," she breathed.

A laugh rumbled in Cade's chest. "Ditto," he said.

Taking the Cake

Mollie opened her eyes to find him smiling at her, a soft glint in his eye. "What?"

"Nothing." He wrapped an arm around her shoulders and started steering her down the walkway. "How are you doing today?"

"Okay." And to her surprise, it was true. She'd expected to be on edge about the whole thing. Been ready to throw in the towel only minutes before Cade arrived. But now that he was here, she felt calm. Determined. Ready to explore her wild side.

They reached the sidewalk and Mollie looked down the street for Cade's car. Maybe he expected her to drive again.

"Here." He thrust a large, rounded object into her hands. She looked down. She was holding a black and yellow helmet.

"Excuse me?"

Cade pulled on a matching helmet and nodded at her hands. "Better put that on. I don't take anyone for a ride without one."

"We're riding a motorcycle?" To her dismay, her voice had inched up until she was approaching dog whistle territory.

He slung one leg over the seat of his motorcycle and twisted around, patting the seat behind him. "Hop on, wild woman." He flashed her that grin that made her knees go wobbly.

Heart pounding, she slid the helmet on and gingerly straddled the bike. "What am I supposed to hold on to?"

Cade reached back and wrapped his hands around hers, pulling her arms forward until they circled his waist. "Hold on to me, sweetheart," he growled, and turned the key. The motorcycle rumbled to life, and Mollie clung to Cade as they roared off to adventure.

ಸಿಂಡ

Sheer torture.

What had he been thinking, putting Mollie on his bike this morning? Even in her circus-clown-sized vehicle they'd have a little space between them. Not on his Harley—she was plastered up against him, breasts soft and tantalizing against his back, her arms wrapped around his waist.

Not to mention her legs clutching his in a grip that bordered on painful.

Now, if she had been wrapped around him like that from the front, it would be a different story.

But knowing she was that close, feeling every inch of her burning into every inch of him, and not being able to do a damn thing about it?

Cade kicked his speed up a notch and angled into the turn. If he didn't get to their destination soon, he'd go stark raving mad.

Hell, he was halfway there already.

He breathed a sigh of relief as the entrance to the park came into view. Spying a parking space near the walking path, he pulled to a stop and killed the engine.

Mollie slid off the bike, her legs looking more than a little shaky after their ride. She pulled off the helmet and shook her head, tossing her hair into place. "I survived!" she crowed, a wide grin on her face.

Cade winked at her and slung a knapsack over his shoulder. "Of course you did. Don't tell me you doubt my driving ability?"

Mollie punched him softly in the shoulder. "I wouldn't doubt anything about you, Cade."

Wow. He cleared his throat and headed for safer territory. "So, did you enjoy your first ride on a Harley?"

She mock-frowned at him. "What makes you think it was my first time?"

He laughed at that, leading her down the path. "The death grip you had on my waist was an indication."

"Oh. Sorry."

"Don't be." He turned back and winked again. "You can hold onto me that tight anytime you want, honey."

She squeaked at that, putting another smile on his face. Man, if he spent more time with her, he'd be facing a state of perma-grin.

"Here we are," he announced, sweeping his arm to indicate the view.

"Wow."

They stood on a cliff overlooking Puget Sound, the Olympic Mountains in the distance. The sun glinted off the choppy water, refracting light in all directions. Tall evergreens ringed the clearing.

Cade opened his pack and took out a blanket, spreading it out on the ground. Then he removed a white paper bag and two no-spill travel cups. He handed one to her. "Always start the day with breakfast."

Mollie took a sip and moaned in delight. "Caramel latte," she exclaimed. "You're going to spoil me."

That's the plan, he thought, but only smiled and held out the bag.

She peeked inside and started to shake her head. "No, I couldn't," she said.

Cade pushed the bag forward again. "Rule number one. No calorie counting. Bad girls enjoy their food, and a little deep-fried heaven is the perfect start to a wild day."

Eyeing him carefully, Mollie reached into the bag and pulled out a doughnut. "Oh, man, are these still warm?"

"Fresh from the fryer, ma'am," he mumbled around his first bite. The sweet pastry dissolved in his mouth, teasing his tastebuds. But the impact of the doughnut paled in comparison to Mollie's reaction.

She sighed. She moaned. She opened her mouth wide for another bite. Then she swallowed, darting her little pink tongue out to lap up a speck of glazing that had dropped at the edge of her mouth.

Cade bit his tongue to keep from helping her with the task.

Together, they finished off the doughnuts in record time, then sat side by side on the blanket, watching the sailboats frisk across the water below.

"So tell me about this list." Cade reached over and twined a lock of her hair around his finger. It was soft and silky and cool to the touch. The spark that flared in her eyes, though, was anything but cool.

"It's nothing." A hint of color stained her cheeks. "Forget I said anything."

He'd love to see if that same blush was visible on other parts of her body. "C'mon, spill."

She sat back, tucking the strands of honey blonde hair behind her ear. It was loose today, spilling around her shoulders in a tumble of gold. He wanted to see it spread out on a pillow, her eyes half-closed with desire. Or draping over his chest as she straddled him, taking him deep inside.

God, he had it bad.

"Okay, fine," she finally grumbled, digging in her purse for a folded piece of paper. Smoothing it out, she handed it to him, then busied herself cleaning up the remnants of their breakfast picnic.

Cade scanned the computer-printed list, biting the inside of his cheek to keep from smiling. Somehow, he knew she wouldn't take kindly to a humorous reaction.

The list was classic Mollie, though. Trust her to turn a walk on the wild side into a structured event. Even in this, she didn't want to leave out a step.

"Hmmm..." He tapped the list against his lower lip. "I'm not so sure about this."

She grabbed for the paper, but he held it just out of reach.

"I know, it was a stupid idea." She rose up on her knees, still trying to take it away from him.

Cade stuffed the list in his back pocket and, in a swift move that left her gasping, pulled her down onto the blanket. He straddled her, knees on either side of her hips, holding her wrists in a loose grip next to her ears. "Not stupid. You could never be stupid."

"Cade," she hissed, wriggling under him. "Someone could see."

"Doubtful." He grinned down at her. "But even if they did, wouldn't that be pretty wild?"

That stopped her protests, half-hearted though they had been. And he could pinpoint the exact moment she realized his body's reaction to their proximity. "Cade," she breathed, but this time, the pleading held a completely different note.

"Now, there's a time and place for lists," he continued, as if he didn't have the king of all boners pressing into the vee of her thighs. "Planning and organizing are important skills."

"I've always thought so," she sighed, hips tilting up for better contact.

"But sometimes," he breathed in her ear, "you just have to feel."

Her breasts rose and fell in a rapid pattern, her heartbeat throbbing in the hollow of her neck. Cade felt his erection swell even more, pressing insistently against the seam of his jeans.

"So tell me, Miss Mollie." He rocked slowly against her hips. "What do you feel?"

She sucked in a breath, eyes wide and unblinking. "Nervous," she said. "Excited. A little scared."

Cade frowned, pulling back. "I'm not trying to scare you," he said.

"No!" Mollie arched up, bringing them back into contact. "I'm not scared of you," she panted. "Never you."

"Then what?" He slid back down, bracing his arms to keep his weight off her. "What are you afraid of?"

She swallowed and turned her head away. "I'm scared of me, of what I might find out."

"What do you mean?"

She was silent for a moment, eyes averted. "What if Blaine is right? What if I am everything he said I was?"

"Don't." He slid his hands down the length of her arms, stroking inward to cup her breasts, smooth the curve of her waist, the flare of her hips. He pressed a kiss to the base of her neck. "Don't give that jerk any more power over you. There's a wild woman inside you just dying to get out. Hell, anyone who jumps out of a cake at a bachelor party on a dare can't be repressed."

"But what if..."

He cut her off with a short, hard kiss. "No what ifs. Just go with it, Mollie. Try on your wild side for size, see how it fits who you want to be. You'll always be you, no matter how wild you might get. Inside..." He placed one hand over her heart. "Right here, you'll always be exactly the same."

With a sound that was halfway between a laugh and a sob, she reached up and threw her arms around his neck, pulling him down on top of her. "Thank you," she murmured, before taking his mouth in a shattering kiss.

Cade briefly pondered the delights of making love outside, but through sheer force of will ended the kiss before it escalated. "Couple of things," he said, rolling off her and flinging one arm across his eyes.

"Yeah?" She snuggled closer. Her fingertips traced patterns on his chest through his T-shirt.

God, he hated bringing this up. "It's about Blaine," he finally spit out.

The patterns stopped. "Blaine," she repeated dully. "Do we have to talk about him?"

He grabbed her hand, bringing her fingertips to his mouth. He nipped at them each in turn, eliciting a soft gasp from her. "I know, sweetheart. I feel the same way. But I just have to know where things stand between you two."

Mollie tugged her hand free and sat up, outrage on her face. "How can you ask that after what he did last night?"

"I know that. You know that. But does he know that?"

She sighed, the anger evaporating like air from a popped balloon. "I tried to call him this morning. But all I got was his voice mail. It just didn't seem like the kind of message you'd want to leave after the beep, you know?"

Cade sat up too, shoving his hands through his hair. "You have to tell him, sweetheart."

"I know." Her face was drawn and pale; he wished there was something, anything, he could do to help. "It's just so—humiliating."

"No." When she wouldn't look at him, he gently grasped her chin and turned her face to his. "He's the loser in this, Mollie. Don't forget that."

She seemed to inflate a little with that, and her expression took on a new resolve. "You're right," she said, getting to her feet. "Let's go."

"Go?"

Mollie reached down and picked up the picnic blanket, folding it into a neat little square. "I need to go end things with Blaine."

"Right now?" Cade stuffed the trash in his backpack; he'd dump it in the garbage can in the parking lot. "Are you sure?"

She stretched up on her tiptoes and planted a hot, tongue-tangling kiss on him, pulling away only when he was ready to toss her down on the grass and to hell with the consequences. "Absolutely," she murmured against his lips. Then she skipped a few steps away, a wicked grin on her face. "I plan on having my way with you, Cade Gallagher. And I want to be free and clear when it happens."

He couldn't help it; his jaw dropped. And, of course, other body parts stood up and cheered. "Well, okay then," he said. Slinging his pack over his shoulder, he nudged her with his elbow. "Race you back to the bike."

And with a shout of laughter, she took him up on the dare.

ஐരു

"Damn." Mollie flipped her phone shut and stuffed it in her purse.

"Problems?" Cade leaned against his bike, arms crossed over his chest.

Mollie sighed, shoving a hand through her hair. What the hell, it was beyond redemption at this point anyway. "Blaine's in a meeting all morning. His secretary told me I could join him for lunch."

"I see."

"So what do we do now?" Mollie checked her watch, feeling at loose ends. Normally at work right now, she had taken the week off to prepare for the wedding and had seen no reason to change her plans just because the wedding wasn't happening.

Besides, it gave her plenty of time for her new project—exploring her wild side with her own personal bad boy.

She still couldn't believe that Cade Gallagher had actually agreed to her crazy plan. But she wasn't about to complain.

And she couldn't wait to take their lessons to the next level.

It was too bad he was only in town for a few weeks, she thought as he helped her adjust her helmet. A girl could get used to this kind of care and attention.

But that was the problem. Just when she'd be getting used to it, he'd be moving on. There was no way a good girl like her could keep the attention of a wild man like Cade. For a few weeks, sure; the novelty of it all would keep him around. But once the newness had worn off, he'd be gone.

At least this way she was aware of the expiration date. And when it was over, she'd have some incredible memories to steam up her lonely nights.

Cade slipped his own helmet on, flashing her that grin that never failed to make her heart rate soar. "Are you up for a change in plans?"

She thought of her list, now tucked in the back pocket of Cade's tight-fitting jeans. Any plans she'd developed last night were now totally in his hands.

Right where she wanted to be.

"Absolutely," she said, almost startling herself with the conviction ringing in her voice.

He straddled the bike, then twisted around to make sure she was settled. "Then hold on, honey, because you're in for a treat."

Chapter Four

"Shopping?" Mollie slid off the bike into Cade's waiting arms, staring at the entryway to the upscale department store. "You actually want to take me shopping?"

"Do you have a problem with that?" Cade took off his helmet, then helped Mollie with hers.

"I'm just surprised, that's all." She shrugged. "Most guys would rather have elective root canal work than spend the day watching a woman shop."

"I'm not most guys."

No kidding. Mollie resisted the urge to roll her eyes at that. Women walking by on the sidewalk were practically giving themselves whiplash checking him out. She'd caught a few incredulous looks tossed her way as well, as if they couldn't believe a guy like Cade was with a woman like her.

She raised her chin a little. *Let* them sneer. *She* got to spend time with him.

Cade took her hand and led the way to the front doors of the store. "Now, if you're going to be a wild woman, you have to dress the part."

She blinked a little at the change in lighting, her eyes adjusting quickly. Soft piano music played in the background, and well-dressed salespeople were stationed throughout the store. "I don't think we're in the right place," she murmured.

"Why not?"

"This is where I usually shop." She waved a hand at her khaki-pants-and-sweater outfit. "Not very wild, I'm afraid."

"Then you've just been in the wrong department. Trust me."

And since she did, Mollie pushed aside all her reservations and settled back to enjoy the experience.

෴

By the fourth outfit Cade had decided he had latent masochistic tendencies.

Mollie had been reticent at first, almost shy about showing off the clothes she was trying on, but with each outfit she'd grown more confident.

God, it was such a turn on.

Of course, Cade suspected that watching her read e-mail would be a turn on.

"I'm not sure about this one," she said, her voice muffled by the closed door of the dressing room.

"I'm sure you look stunning." The leather armchair creaked as he shifted, impatient to see the next outfit. "Come on out."

"All right."

He could hear a huff of impatience, and bit back a smile.

The door swung open, and she stepped out of the dressing room. Turning in a slow circle, she said, "Okay, what's your verdict?"

For long moments, Cade said nothing at all, mostly because all his blood had rushed out of his head and traveled south. Immediately.

Like the other outfits she'd modeled for him this morning, the dress was ostensibly proper, something she could wear to work or a social function with ease. But instead of the full slacks and business-like tops she was prone to wear, this emphasized every one of her considerable assets.

The sleeveless dress was short and flirty, with a skirt that ended well above the knees. It nipped in close at her waist, and flared over her hips. The top was close-fitting and just low-cut enough to highlight her mouth-watering cleavage. Thin straps completed the look.

"There's a matching jacket," the saleswoman interjected, but Cade stopped her with a raised hand.

"No," he said quietly, eyes focused on Mollie. "It's perfect."

The saleswoman wisely chose that moment to excuse herself, heading for the back room to collect more items for Mollie to try.

A blush rose in Mollie's cheeks, adding a fresh bloom that went well with the floral print of her dress. "You're sure it's not too...revealing?"

"There's no doubt that it's sexy, but not over-the-top. You could wear this to lunch with your grandmother and be perfectly appropriate." He couldn't resist a little leer. "But if you brought me along, you might have to worry about being accosted in the kitchen."

Her blush grew even brighter. "I'll keep that in mind," she murmured.

"Do you like it?" He waved a hand at the dress. "I think it looks great, but you're the one who'll be wearing it."

"Yeah, I don't think it'd fit you." She grinned. "I do like it. I like everything you've picked out so far. I should let you dress me all the time."

He shut his eyes briefly at the thought of slowly putting clothes on her, one piece at a time.

"I have to admit, I'm a bit surprised at the choices you made." She glanced at the dressing room, where several more outfits awaited her. "They're great, but I guess I expected them to be a bit more…"

"Trampy?" He smiled to take the edge out of the statement. "You don't have to dress like a hooker to explore the wild side. These are just a sexier version of what you usually wear, so they just push your comfort zone a bit rather than destroying it. You'll be more likely to actually wear them this way, too."

"That makes sense. I feel like a wimp, though."

"Hell, Mollie, you look incredibly sexy. This dress makes your legs look ten miles long, and I don't even want to think about your breasts."

"Uh, okay…"

He surged out of his chair and walked over to her, leaning down to whisper in her ear. "I don't want to think of them because if I do, we'll never finish this shopping trip."

The saleswoman chose that moment to return, carrying several new outfits. Cade stepped away and settled back into his chair. "Go on. I'll be right here."

And as she walked away, he admitted to himself that he couldn't think of anywhere else he'd want to be.

ഓഃ

The click of the door closing was her first clue that she wasn't alone.

"What are you doing in here?" Mollie snatched up a discarded blouse from the floor of the changing room and held it in front of her. "I'm changing!"

Cade reached out and took the blouse from her, prying it out of her fingers before draping it on the overstuffed chair in the corner of the tiny room. "Miss me?"

Mollie crossed her arms over her chest, trying to hide the fact that she was wearing only a silk camisole and high-cut panties.

"Nice," Cade said in a low murmur, taking the strap of the camisole between thumb and forefinger and rubbing the material gently. "Yours?"

She shook her head. "The saleswoman thought they'd be a good foundation for the outfits. And speaking of her, you'd better get out of here before she finds you."

He just grinned. "She's off hunting for more clothes for you. And the thrill of possibly being discovered is half the fun." He moved even closer, running a hand down her side, smoothing the sleek fabric against her overheated skin.

His hand slipped lower, toying with the edge of her panties. "I'm afraid you're going to have to buy these," he said, shaking his head sadly.

"Why?" She arched into his touch, too focused on his butterfly-light strokes to worry about much of anything anymore.

"Can't return them now." He eased one finger under the edge of the panties, teasing the curls that lay underneath.

She sucked in a breath, twisting under his delicate touch.

"In fact, you might want to wear them out of here," he continued. "It wouldn't do to return damp panties, would it?"

"No," she gasped as he stroked the sensitive flesh. "It wouldn't do at all."

He withdrew his hand, leaving her aching and frustrated, but instead of walking away, he turned her so her back was to him. He stepped forward, pulling her hips back until he was pressed against her backside. His erection nestled against her, sending a thrill of heat right to her center. She closed her eyes, dropping her head back onto his shoulder.

"No, sweetheart," he murmured, his fingers toying with the lacy edge of her panties. "Open your eyes. I want you to watch."

Startled, her eyes flew open. For the first time, she realized they were standing directly in front of the mirrors. The three mirrors reflected their images from every angle. Her honey blonde hair, mussed and tangled, draped across his wide shoulder. Her blue eyes looked slumberous and heavy with desire. Her legs were spread open, her arms loose at her sides.

Cade stood behind her, his solid form dwarfing her smaller figure, his tanned darkness contrasting with her pale skin. His eyes maintaining contact with hers in the front mirror, he slowly slid one hand inside the waistband of her silk panties.

Still watching, still darkly intent, he slid one finger inside her, triumph flashing in his chocolate eyes as she bit back a moan. His other hand eased under the hem of her camisole, tickling her stomach, trailing up her ribs, over the swell of her breast to roll one sensitive nipple between thumb and forefinger. With gentle determination, he stroked and plucked it to aching tightness, then moved across to its twin.

His finger slid in and out while his thumb traced delicate circles around her clitoris. She gasped again as a second finger joined the first, filling and stretching her.

"Watch," he said again, his voice tense with strain. The hard length of his erection pressed against her silk-covered bottom, and she rotated her hips almost unconsciously, pulling a ragged groan from his throat.

Her strength seemed to disappear, and she gripped his thighs with her hands, knowing only his touch was keeping her upright. He worked his fingers in and out, faster and faster, keeping constant eye contact with her through the mirrors. She watched, distantly fascinated, as the blonde woman she barely recognized as herself panted and writhed in his embrace. Suddenly, the tension reached a breaking point, and her orgasm washed over her, pulling a cry from her mouth.

Cade turned his head and kissed her, swallowing her cries of release as she shook in his arms. Slowly, teasingly, he withdrew his hands, turned her, and eased her to a seat in the corner chair. Then he knelt before her, straightening her lingerie and soothing the trembling muscles of her legs. He pressed a kiss to her forehead and turned to go, stripping off his leather jacket and looping it around his waist, the crossed arms hiding the evidence of his arousal. "Try the red outfit next," he suggested. "You'll look totally hot in it."

"Cade, I—" She stared at him, unsure what to say.

He smiled and leaned forward, gripping her shoulders gently as he kissed her briefly on the lips. "Now, when you're saying goodbye to Blaine, you'll be thinking of this, not the stupid lies he told about you." Then he slipped out of the room.

In a daze, Mollie pulled the red outfit off the hanger and slipped it on. She had a feeling it would be a long time before she would be able to think about anything else at all.

℘Ƈ

The noise and heat of the restaurant hit her like a physical blow as she opened the door. Stomach clenching, she stopped, taking a deep breath to calm her nerves.

Softly, a hand stroked the bare skin of her neck. Cade leaned close and whispered in her ear. "You can do this."

She leaned back as he gently rubbed the tension out of her neck and shoulders. He was right. She *could* do this. Her nervous tension drained away, Cade's touch filling her with resolve. More than that—it set nerve endings ablaze, making her nipples tighten and heat rush between her legs. Even this simple, casual touch was a blatant reminder of their intimate encounter in the dressing room.

For a minute, the rush of sexual desire was so strong she thought her legs would fail her. Then his grip tightened, pulling her close. "I'll be right here if you need me. Now go make a scene, wild woman." His hot breath raised goose bumps on the sensitive skin of her neck, making her shiver. He pressed an open-mouth kiss to her neck, tickling the skin with his tongue. With a low laugh, he let go and stepped back.

Mollie looked over her shoulder and flashed him a grin. Now that she was over her minor anxiety attack, she was almost looking forward to the confrontation. Turning to face him, she looked around to make sure no one was watching, then quickly unbuttoned her jacket and flashed him a peek at her lacy camisole. From the spark of heat that flamed to life in his eyes, she knew he liked what he saw. Buttoning it up again, she reveled in the strength of his desire, a desire he made no attempt to hide.

"Go call off the wedding officially so I can take you home and have my way with you," he growled, eyes hot with need.

She winked at him and walked into the restaurant, leaving him to wait in the entryway. With a confident stride, she waved off the hostess and continued on into the seating area.

Blaine was sitting at their usual table, his back to her. Several of his friends were crowded around, drinking beer and huddling over the tabletop. As she approached, she could see that they were passing around a thong, obviously a memento from the night before.

A surge of anger swept through her, bolstering her resolve. She came to a stop right behind his chair. "Hello, Blaine."

"Hey, Mol," he said, not even looking at her, as he stuffed the thong into his pocket. Did he think she was blind? Of course, considering the discussion she'd overheard the night before, she supposed he did. He waved a hand behind him, motioning her forward. "Grab a seat."

"No, thanks. I'd rather stand." It went without saying that she had no desire to spend any more time with him than necessary.

He swiveled around in his chair. "Too much wedding stuff to do, huh?" Then he did a double take, eyes bulging out as he took in her outfit. "Jesus, Mollie, what the hell are you wearing?"

His buddies turned around at that. Junior, in the middle of taking a drink of his beer, spewed it across the table. Mollie lifted one eyebrow. "I'll take that as a compliment," she said.

Blaine stood up, stripping off his suit jacket as he rose. "Put this on," he ordered.

"No," she said simply. And had to bite back a grin at his look of astonishment.

Truthfully, she wasn't surprised at his reaction. Her outfit was a definite departure from her normal look. Not to mention her attitude adjustment.

They were starting to draw looks from the other tables, Blaine trying to cover her up, Mollie sidestepping his attempts. In the past, she would have been horrified at being the center of attention, but today she welcomed it. It was time to take back some of the power she'd abdicated to him for so long.

"The wedding's off." She crossed her arms over her chest. The motion lifted her cleavage, accentuating the lace-covered curves exposed by the low cut, form-fitting red jacket. "Have a nice life." She turned to go, then wrenched her arm out of his grasp as he grabbed at her elbow.

"You can't be serious." He laughed nervously. A quick glance verified that everyone at the table was listening avidly to their conversation. "Look, everybody gets cold feet. Let's go somewhere and talk privately."

"Why?" She shot him a contemptuous look. "You sure didn't mind an audience last night."

"What are you talking about?" He took a step back.

She glanced at the people watching them. "You know, you don't even deserve this much courtesy. I should have just left you waiting at the altar. But I have a little more integrity than that. And I wanted you to know that I am not oblivious. I am not married to my career. And I am most definitely not frigid. So you can go ahead and enjoy your playtime with all the strippers you want, and find yourself some other doormat to build up your image."

If his jaw dropped any lower, it'd be dragging on the ground. "I don't know who the hell told you that, but it's a lie. Come on, baby, you know you can't believe everything you hear." He reached out again, but she moved out of his reach.

"True. But you can believe what you see." She reached into his jacket pocket and pulled out the thong. "Nice souvenir. Maybe you can get another one at your next bachelor party. But

Taking the Cake

I'd recommend that the next time a girl jumps out of a cake, you pay attention. It just might be someone you know." Then she blew a kiss to the guys at the table, sang out, "Later, boys," and sauntered back out of the room.

ಸಂ

Cade had just about decided to charge in after her when Mollie appeared. Her face was flushed and her eyes sparkled. She looked around the lobby, her expression brightening as she saw him.

He went instantly hard as she sashayed toward him, her long legs shown off to perfection in that barely-there red miniskirt he'd recommended at the store. Christ, what had he been thinking? Every man in a ten-mile radius had to be sporting wood just from looking at her.

Her top was just as magnificent, with her lush figure showcased in lace peeking out from under the nipped-in jacket. And he'd gotten a sneak peek of just what that lace looked like without the jacket on top to keep her outfit from being completely carnal.

He'd been semi-hard ever since.

Oh, who was he kidding? There was nothing semi about it.

"I did it!" She wrapped her arms around his neck and squeezed him tight. The three-inch heels put her in perfect alignment with him, and he bit back a groan as she brushed against his jeans-straining erection.

"Congrats," he said. Now how long did he have to wait before taking her to bed? She'd just gotten out of a bad relationship. And yeah, she'd picked him to be her rebound guy, but he didn't want to push her too hard and blow it now. He'd

61

been waiting for a decade; a little longer wasn't going to kill him.

Theoretically.

She snuggled in closer and nipped at the underside of his jaw. "Take me home," she murmured.

"Sure." He stomped down his disappointment. "You probably need some down time." He wrapped one arm around her shoulders and steered her out of the restaurant. The sidewalk outside was full of people enjoying the late-afternoon sunshine.

"No, I think you misunderstood." She bumped her hip against his as they walked. "I don't want you to take me to my home. I want you to take me to *yours.*"

His heart skipped a beat, then started hammering double-time. "Are you sure?"

She wrapped her arm around his waist, stroking his hip, then tucked her hand in his back pocket and squeezed. His cock grew even harder at her touch. "More sure than I've been in years." Standing on her tiptoes, she nipped his earlobe and whispered, "Cade, I'm ready to be wicked. Are you game?"

"Hell, yes!" In deference to her outfit, they'd switched to the Bug before coming to the restaurant. Now he held out his free hand for her keys. "I'll drive."

৪০০৪

They hit every stop light on the way through town.

Mollie squirmed in her seat. She cast a surreptitious look at Cade, sitting calmly in the seat next to her. He was a casual driver, one elbow resting on the open window frame, one finger hooked on the steering wheel. His other hand rested on her knee, tracing delicate patterns on her sensitized skin.

As if he felt her eyes on him, he tilted his head in her direction. One side of his mouth lifted in a lazy, sensual smile. Then he trailed one finger up the inside of her leg right to the hem of her skirt.

It was a very, very short skirt.

She sucked in a breath, her stomach going into free fall mode.

"Ticklish?" His voice was low and rough, suggesting that he wasn't quite as cavalier about this as she first thought.

Mollie shook her head, barely able to form words, much less vocalize them. His finger stroked her leg at the edge of her skirt, just missing the top of her thigh-high stockings.

He glanced over at her again, blatantly checking out her breasts. "Maybe a little—cold?"

Mollie felt a blush rise in her cheeks, aware that her nipples were beading against her jacket top. "Excited," she said boldly.

"Me, too," he confessed. He took her hand and pressed it against the crotch of his jeans. "See for yourself."

Even through the denim fabric she could feel the heat and hardness of him. Hesitant and excited at the same time, she stroked her fingertips up the full length of his cock, thrilled when he groaned and arched into her touch. Emboldened, she used a harder stroke. He twitched under her palm.

"Bad idea." He grabbed her wrist and dragged her hand away from his lap. "Any more of that and I'll drive your Bug off the road."

"Can't have that," she murmured. "Drive faster."

"No problem." He lifted his hand from her leg to shift gears, then placed it back on her thigh, inching underneath the hem of her skirt. His fingers stilled at the edge of her stockings. He flashed her a sharp look. "Are you wearing a garter?"

She smoothed the fabric of the skirt. Under the thin material, the raised outline of her new garter belt was visible. "The saleswoman suggested it."

Cade swallowed. "Remind me to send her a thank you note." Under the skirt, his hand traveled to the telltale ridge, stroking the bare skin above her stocking. "You are so sexy."

She shook her head. "The clothes—" she started, but he cut her off.

"You have always been sexy, Mollie. The clothes just verify what I already knew."

"Since when?" She rolled her eyes. "Yesterday?"

"High school." He slid his hand upward, teasing the edge of her panties. "I used to get hard, just thinking about touching you."

She sucked in a breath, feeling a rush of dampness at his touch. "I didn't even know that you noticed me," she whispered.

"I noticed plenty." One finger slipped under the panty line, stroking her sensitized flesh. "God, Mollie, you're so wet. I can't wait to taste you."

She squirmed, moaning a little. Cade kept his eyes on the road, even while his hand worked magic. "I noticed that sweet little ass swaying just a little as you walked down the hall. I noticed your gorgeous breasts, even when you wore something conservative. I used to wonder what your hair would look like, out of your usual braid, spread out on my pillow."

"Really?" Her voice was high pitched and breathless. "I was just a boring nice girl."

His finger moved upwards, circling her clit. "Don't sell yourself short, Mollie. Nice girls can be walking wet dreams, too."

"Cade, please," she whimpered. "You're torturing me."

"Good." He flashed her a grin, full of promise. "Because you've been torturing me for years."

He withdrew his hand, leaving her on the edge of anticipation.

"We're here." He pulled into the driveway and shut off the engine. Jumping out of the car, he rounded the front and opened her door. "Ready?"

She nodded, stepping carefully out of the car. She wasn't quite used to the heels yet, and falling on her face would put a definite damper on things.

Cade took one look and swung her into his arms, bumping the car door closed with his hip.

"Cade! What are you doing?"

He kissed her. Staked his claim. "I'm not taking any chances." Then with a long, confident stride, he carried her to the house.

Chapter Five

Cade kicked the door shut behind him. The slam echoed through the narrow entryway, but he was too focused on his destination to pay more than cursory attention.

After her initial protest, Mollie had relaxed in his arms, wrapping her arms around his neck and resting her head on his shoulder. He was on the sharp edge of desire right now, balanced precariously. But below the sexual tension lay another, sweeter sensation.

It had always been more than a desire for sex where Mollie was concerned, though he wouldn't lie and say he hadn't wanted her. But she only wanted a no-strings affair, an exploration of her wild side. And he'd better remember that before he did something completely stupid and fell in love with her.

Or let her know that he already had.

"This is your dad's house?" She lifted her head and looked around. "I've never been here before. It's nice."

"Thanks." *No one* had been to his house back when he was in high school. His dad had never taken an interest in restoring the old Craftsman-style home, especially after his mom took off when he was in elementary school. Since his dad died last year, Cade had spent quite a bit of money having the place whipped into shape. It had never looked this good when he was growing up.

Truthfully, he'd been pretty shocked when he walked in for the first time a few weeks ago. It was amazing what a boatload of money could do. If he'd been practical, he would have sold it right away and cut his losses. It wasn't as if the area held much appeal.

He looked down at the warm, pliant woman in his arms. This was one of the biggest draws, right here.

"You can put me down now." She twisted in his arms. In response, he tightened his grip, holding her so close he could feel her nipples rasping against his chest.

"I want to carry you," he said. "Believe me, it's fulfilling quite a few fantasies."

"Really?" She sounded intrigued. "Tell me about them."

"I don't know," he said. "Seems a bit one-sided, me spilling all my deep dark secrets."

"Fair enough." She snuggled closer again. "You tell me one, and I'll tell you one of mine."

"Deal." They reached the door to the master suite, and he shouldered it open, thankful he'd taken the time to straighten up this morning. He set her down on the king-sized bed, bending down to unbuckle her shoes. He lifted one up and inspected it. "You know what these are, don't you?"

"Uh, shoes?" She raised her eyebrows at him, the picture of innocence.

He smirked at her. "They're called fuck-me pumps," he said. "Unofficially, of course."

She levered herself up on her elbows. "No way."

"Way." He slipped off the other one. "They do amazing things to your legs and ass, make you look like sex personified. Major turn-on."

"Thanks." She sucked in a breath as he stroked her instep. "But you're avoiding the subject."

"No I'm not." He slid his palms up her calves, rounding to tease the backs of her knees. "I'm living it."

"Oh," she breathed.

"I'd carry you to my room, lay you out on the bed, and slowly undress you." His fingers fumbled with the fasteners of her garters, finally working the stockings free. He curved his forefingers in the lace at the top of one stocking and slowly drew it down her leg, taking pleasure in the shivers that followed the path of his fingers. He did the same with the other, dropping it on the hardwood floor. Hooking his thumbs in the sides of her panties, he pulled them off, adding them to the little pile of lingerie at his feet. Then he grasped her knees and pulled her down the bed, until she was situated right at the edge, her toes brushing the floor. "You're even more beautiful than I imagined," he whispered before dropping to his knees between her legs.

The first sweep of his tongue nearly brought her off the bed, but he merely draped his arms over her thighs and settled in for another taste.

She was sweet, both in the taste of her and in the way she squirmed and panted under his touch. He laved her with his tongue, rasping gently over her clit while he worked one finger inside. Stroking in and out, building in rhythm, he worked her to the edge until she exploded, her head tossing from side to side as she gasped her release. Inner muscles clamped around his finger, pushing him close to coming himself.

Standing, he started to unbutton his shirt, but only managed to undo half the buttons before she sat up and placed a hand on his chest. "Stop."

He dropped his hands. "You okay?"

"Better than okay." She stroked her hand under the open edge of his shirt, touching his bare skin. "But turnabout is fair play. You told me your fantasy. Now I want to tell you mine."

She sucked in a breath at the feel of his heated skin under her fingers. Her body was still quivering with little aftershocks, aching for more. It had never been like this before, and it scared her a little. Somehow, this had become more than just a casual affair, at least as far as she was concerned.

"I noticed you, too. I mean, back in high school."

"You don't have to say that."

She shot him a quelling look. "I don't lie." Grabbing the front of his shirt, she turned him until his knees hit the bed. He sat down next to her. "And I did notice you. Every day. You'd walk past in the hall, and it was all I could do not to stare."

"I never knew."

She shrugged and pushed on his shoulders, urging him onto his back. He lay down, moving back until his head was on the pillows. She swung one leg over his waist, straddling him. He was so hard, a thick ridge at the fly of his jeans pressing against her sensitive flesh.

"Believe me, I had to work hard to hide it." She undid the rest of his buttons, spreading the fabric wide and exposing his chest. "No one filled out a pair of jeans like you did."

"Why thank you. I think." He levered his hips up to press against her.

She almost strangled on the combination of laugh and moan. "I used to watch you and wonder what it would be like to be with you. But I never thought I stood a chance with all the babes hanging around."

"Selling yourself short again?" He reached up and cupped her breasts, thumbs teasing her taut nipples. "Bad habit."

"I'll work on it." She leaned into his touch.

"Good. Now tell me the rest of your fantasy."

"It's after school." She unbuttoned her jacket and stripped it off, leaving her lacy camisole. "Everyone's gone home, and the halls are dark."

He traced her areoles, visible through the lacy fabric. "Sounds good to me."

"Mmm." She wriggled against his erection. "I'm standing at my locker when you walk by. You see me there and stop to talk. Then you press me up against the locker bank and kiss me."

"Better and better." He urged her down, his palm cupping the back of her neck, and kissed her deeply.

Breaking away, she rolled off him and went to work on his jeans. "Then you take my hand and lead me into the green room of the theater, you know, the one with the big overstuffed couch?"

"I remember."

"You lay me down on the couch and make love to me," she said, finally getting his fly undone.

He surged to his knees, reaching behind her to unzip her skirt. He helped her wriggle out of it, then gripped the hem of her camisole and stripped it off over her head.

"You're wearing too many clothes," she complained, pulling his shirt off and running her palms over his wide chest.

Grinning, he stood, shucking his jeans and boxers in one fluid movement, then reached over to his nightstand and retrieved a foil packet. Ripping it open, he sheathed himself, took her shoulders and pressed her down until she was lying on her back.

She sucked in a breath, reveling in his strength and obvious enthusiasm. He straddled her, finger-combing her hair so it spread across his pillows.

"Nice," he said softly, a gentle look in his eye. "Even better than I imagined."

Her heart ached at his tenderness. He pressed a kiss to her lips, then inched backward so he was between her legs. Lifting her hips, he slid into her slowly.

She groaned, inner muscles relaxing to accommodate him. He filled her completely, setting off little tremors as she neared orgasm again.

Cade stopped, arms braced to hold his weight off her. "You feel so good," he rasped. "I don't think I can last for much longer."

Mollie slid her hands down to cup his buttocks. "Then don't," she said, urging him closer.

As if a switch had been flipped, he began to move. He pulled back, surging into her again on the downstroke. He moved faster and faster, muscles trembling as he thrust into her.

She lifted her legs and wrapped them around his waist, giving him deeper access. With each thrust, she rose up to meet him, feeling delicious tension spiraling through her.

Then she shattered in his arms, trembling and moaning as she came. Cade gave one final thrust, burying himself deeply in her, before collapsing on her with a hoarse shout.

Long moments passed, both of them breathing heavily, wrapped in each other's arms. Mollie ran her fingers through his hair and over his shoulders, memorizing the feel of him, the scent, the taste. If she never had another chance with Cade, she wanted to hold the memory close.

Turning her head away, she blinked back sudden tears. Maybe she wasn't cut out for a casual affair. She'd set the ground rules, wanting to explore her wild side, but she had no desire to be wild with anyone else.

Unfortunately, Cade wasn't going to be around much longer. And once he left, she'd be worse off than she had been before.

Now she knew just what she'd been missing for so many years.

ଛେଓ

Cade paced around his tiny kitchen, pulling food out of the fridge and off shelves, and roundly cursed himself.

He'd pushed too hard, too fast, and now she was having second thoughts.

Something had changed after they'd made love. She'd tried to hide it, but he couldn't miss her lapse into quietness, or the sheen of tears on her lashes.

Please don't let her regret this, he thought, taking out a loaf of bread and slapping it down on the counter.

"You have something against carbs?" She stood uncertainly in the doorframe, wearing only his discarded button-down shirt. It hit her at mid-thigh, accentuating her long, slim legs and bare feet.

He already wanted her again.

"Hmmm?" He'd lost the thread of conversation the minute he saw her.

She gestured at the flattened loaf. "That poor bread never did anything to you."

He smiled at her tentative joke and turned back to the fridge. "Thought you might be hungry." He took out some sliced turkey. "Sorry I don't have anything really substantial."

"Sandwiches are fine," she said, coming into the kitchen. "The house is amazing, by the way."

"Thanks." He held up two sodas, lifting his eyebrows in silent question. She pointed to the diet, which he handed to her. They both sat down at the table and began to put together sandwiches, tension thick in the air around them.

Damn, she *was* having second thoughts. He'd blown it bigtime.

Mollie swallowed her bite of sandwich, then cleared her throat. "Uh, Cade," she began, and his heart sank. "I just wanted to say...thank you."

Cade shook his head. "Please don't."

"What?"

"Don't thank me. I didn't do this as a favor."

Mollie shifted in her seat. "I didn't mean to insult you."

"No insult taken. If anything, you were insulting yourself, and you shouldn't. I made love with you because I wanted to—because I wanted *you*, and to think otherwise is just wrong. You are a beautiful, sexy, desirable woman, and I'd keep you in my bed for the next week if I could."

"Two," she said softly.

His head snapped up. "Excuse me?"

Mollie stood, undoing her top button. "You'd better make it two. I'm not expected back at work until then."

What was he going to say to that? "Oh, hell, yeah."

She smiled, flirting with the next button, revealing the swell of her breast, naked under his button-down shirt. "And I think those two weeks should start as soon as possible."

Cade dropped his sandwich and surged to his feet, body straining with need. Rounding the table, he gripped her sweet little ass and lifted her tight against him, her cleft aligned with his erection. "Well okay then," he said before taking her mouth in a passionate kiss.

He rocked against her until she pulled back, eyes bright with desire. She slid her hands down the back of his cutoff sweats, taking a moment to squeeze his ass before skimming them off, leaving him naked and fully erect.

"Mollie," he groaned, but she just smiled, reaching down to stroke him.

Her touch was light, hesitant at first, then growing bolder as he surged into her hand. Her other hand reached below to cup him, as she planted a hot, openmouthed kiss on his chest at the same time.

Cade closed his eyes. The light floral scent of her shampoo drifted around him, her shining blonde hair brushing against his stomach as she dipped lower.

She wasn't really going to…

Mollie put one hand in the center of his chest and pushed, catching him off-guard and dropping him into her abandoned chair. "My turn," she murmured, then sank to her knees between his legs and took him in her mouth.

Her tongue swirled around the broad head, nearly sending him out of the chair. His hands tangled in her hair, cupping the back of her head. Emboldened by his response, she took him deeper into her mouth, tongue stroking the sensitive underside. Her actions sent him almost to the edge, and he knew if he didn't pull back now he'd explode.

"No," he rasped. "I want to be inside you when I come."

Her quick intake of breath told him she was on the edge, too, so he started to stand.

"Where are you going?" Mollie got to her feet, one hand in the center of his chest to keep him in the chair.

"Condom," he ground out, jerking his head at the hall to his bedroom.

"One step ahead of you." She reached into the pocket of her shirt and took out a foil packet.

"I love a woman who's prepared," he said, grabbing for it, but she held it just out of reach.

"Let me." She tore open the packet and sheathed him, then straddled his lap. The tip of his erection brushed against her slick folds, making them both groan. She was hot and wet, more than ready for him, and he pressed up just as she slid down onto him, taking him deep inside.

She stilled, adjusting to his size, panting a little before raising up again.

Cade gripped the edges of her shirt and pulled, popping buttons across the room. He stripped it off her, leaving her completely bare.

"Cade!" Her voice held a breathless mixture of admonishment and laughter. "Your shirt!"

"Never liked that shirt much anyway," he muttered before bending her back over his arm and closing his mouth over one straining nipple.

She cried out, arching into his embrace. He moved to the other side, giving it the same attention, until both nipples were drawn tight.

Wrapping her arms around his neck, she began to move in earnest now, sliding up and down on him with increasing fervor. He moved a hand between their joined bodies, touching her right at the center of her desire.

She gasped, inner muscles clenching around him, and then climaxed, arching and bowing as the tremors shook her.

That was enough to take him over the edge, too, and he groaned her name as he pulsed inside her.

For longer than he cared to admit, they just sat there, breathing heavily. Once he was certain his legs would hold them, Cade stood, still inside her, and started to walk.

"Cade!" Mollie wrapped her legs around him. "Where are you going?"

He nuzzled her neck, pulling a giggle out of her. "Bed," he said, striding down the hall. "Your schedule is full for the next two weeks."

And maybe, if he could just work his way past her time limit, he could convince her that he should be in her life for much, much longer.

Chapter Six

A soft whistle drew Mollie's attention away from her neglected paperwork. Caroline leaned against the doorframe of her office, arms crossed over her chest. Her flame-red hair was pulled back in a businesslike twist, the only concession to her vibrant personality the two take-out chopsticks holding it in place. A lopsided smile brought out the dimple in her peaches and cream complexion.

"You look amazing." Caroline inspected Mollie's new outfit with approval. "Very hot, but businesslike. A definite improvement."

"Gee, thanks," Mollie said dryly, glancing down at the butter yellow linen dress.

"Oh, stop. You know you're gorgeous whatever you wear. It's just that now your clothes look as great as you do. And your hair! Wowza!"

Mollie waved her in, dredging up a smile even though her heart wasn't in it.

Caroline walked in and dropped into the chair across from her desk, leaning forward with a frown. "Uh-oh. That's a fake smile if I ever saw one."

Mollie tapped a button on her phone and told the receptionist to hold her calls. Then she crossed to the door and closed it with a decisive click. "I am such an idiot," she wailed quietly, acutely aware that the walls of this office were anything but soundproofed.

Caroline immediately jumped up again, giving her a quick hug. "What's wrong? You're not having second thoughts about Blaine, are you?"

"No!" She stared at her friend with undisguised horror. "Bite your tongue!"

"Whew." Caroline wiped imaginary sweat off her brow. "You had me worried for a minute."

"I said I was an idiot, not brain dead."

"Then this must be related to your mystery man."

Mollie groaned and dropped back into her chair, covering her face with her hands.

"Damn, I hate being right." Caroline leaned back. "What happened? Do I have to kick his ass?"

"No." Mollie laughed in spite of herself. "If anyone needs an ass-kicking, it's me."

"Okay, spill it."

She sighed, lifting her shoulders in a gesture of defeat. "I can't even manage a torrid affair right," she said. "I thought I could handle it without letting emotions get involved. But they are, and I don't know what to do."

Caroline frowned at her. "Well, of course you couldn't keep your emotions out of it," she said. "I could tell by talking to you the other night that you were halfway in love with him, whoever he is."

"No!" She surged to her feet again. "I can't be. I just like him. A lot. Okay, more than a lot. Dammit!" She planted her hands on her hips. "Why can't you ever be wrong?"

"It's a curse." Caroline waved the question away. "So why not tell him how you feel?"

"Because that's against the ground rules," she said. "Besides, he's only passing through. I knew there was an expiration date on this before it even started."

"So what?"

"So, I don't want to ruin it by getting clingy or making him feel obligated!"

"But what if he wants more, too?"

Mollie stopped, momentarily stumped. "I don't know."

"The way I see it, you've been selling yourself short for far too long. For once, you've been focusing on you—calling off the wedding, finding a new look, starting a hot affair with a hot guy. So now you want more. Well, I say go for it. If he's really leaving, what have you got to lose?"

Mollie shrugged, unable to look her friend in the eye.

"Think about it." Caroline crossed her arms over her chest and eyed Mollie closely. "So who is this mystery guy, anyway?"

"Caroline..."

"Hey, I've been patient. I haven't flipped you shit about your need for secrecy. But as you said, things have gotten serious pretty quickly. I'm just curious to know who the man is who finally captured your heart."

Mollie sighed, her shoulders slumping. "It's Cade."

"Who?" Caroline looked at her, uncomprehending.

"Cade. Cade Gallagher."

"Omigod!" Caroline leapt forward, squealing, to grab Mollie in a rib-crushing hug. "You're kidding!"

"Nope." Despite herself, Mollie grinned weakly at her friend's enthusiasm. "The one and only."

"Oh, man, the fantasies I had about that boy in high school..." Caroline took one look at Mollie's face and started to backtrack. "Had. *Had.* Back off, Jealousy Woman."

Mollie grimaced apologetically. "Sorry."

"You should be. Keeping news like that from me for two whole weeks! I didn't even know he was in town."

"He won't be after tomorrow."

Caroline mock-hit her upside the head. "Now stop that negative talk. If you managed to catch a fine specimen like Cade, you'd better not let him go."

"I'll try."

"You'll do." Caroline checked her watch. "I've got an appointment in a few minutes, but I can be back later today if you want to pencil in that ass-kicking. You definitely deserve it now."

Mollie laughed and waved Caroline out the door. Then she sat at her desk, staring blankly at the spotless surface. Maybe she should take Caroline's advice and tell Cade how she felt.

Or maybe not. The last time she had listened to Caro, she had ended up in a rubber cake dressed like a demented whore.

Of course, she also ended up in Cade's bed. So maybe Caroline's advice was worthwhile, after all.

ಬಡ

Cade clicked off the computer and leaned back in his chair. Everything was on track for his meeting in Dallas; with luck, he'd have the whole project wrapped up in less than two weeks.

After that, though, his life was in chaos.

With each passing day, he knew he was ready to give up the nomadic lifestyle that had defined his existence for the past several years. He wanted to put down roots, have a real home for a change.

A home with Mollie.

They'd spent almost every spare moment together, and not just in bed. They'd explored the city they had both grown up in, enjoying the opportunity to see it from a new perspective, with fresh eyes. Mollie's enthusiasm was contagious, and he found himself warming to places that had held pain for him in the past.

And speaking of warming...

Cade shifted in his seat, the mere thought of Mollie enough to arouse him. He'd agreed to her short-term exploration in the hopes of showing her that they could have so much more. But now that his departure was imminent, he wondered if it had been enough.

Would she be glad their time together was ending? Or would she be open to more?

He picked up the phone and dialed. His plane was leaving in the morning. If he was ever going to find out, it would be tonight.

ಸಿಠಿಧ

Mollie flipped her hair away from her face and fastened an earring, gazing in the mirror. She grimaced at the look on her face—a combination of nervousness and dismay. If this was truly her last night with Cade, she certainly didn't want to leave him with that impression.

She could be calm. Cool. Blasé, even.

She rolled her eyes at her reflection. Yeah, right.

Well, the most she could hope for was "not distraught".

The doorbell rang, sending her heart pounding. Picking up her tiny clutch purse, she walked down the hall to answer the door.

Cade was wearing a suit.

Over the past two weeks she'd seen him in—and out—of most styles of clothing, from jeans and T-shirts to khakis and pullovers, even tossing in a bright-orange swimsuit for variety when they'd visited the local beach on an unseasonably hot day. But this was the first time he'd ever truly dressed up.

It fit him perfectly, emphasizing his broad shoulders and trim waist. He had one hand in his pocket, a smile teasing the edges of his mouth. "Hey."

She breathed a hello, sure her love and desire for him was written in big capital letters across her forehead. "You look great." Understatement of the century, but for some reason she couldn't get her brain to access her vocabulary.

"So do you." He looked her up and down as deliberately as she was checking him out.

She blushed. She'd chosen the short floral dress he'd liked so much in the store, adding strappy sandals and a gauzy wrap against the night air. Underneath, she wore the camisole and panties that had been such a hit that first day, as well as the garter belt and stockings.

Was she trying to put together a greatest hits collection?

"I told you that dress would be perfect."

She fidgeted with the fringed hem of her wrap. "You're sure it's not too..."

"It is definitely 'too'." With a hand to the small of her back, he steered her out the door. "But I'm glad you're wearing it anyway."

It was his turn to drive, so she handed him the keys to the Bug as soon as they got outside, and slid into the passenger seat next to him. She found a radio station playing soft jazz music, and they rode to the restaurant in a companionable silence.

Wrapped in the comfort, though, was a nervous tension she couldn't quite shake. How could she tell him she wasn't ready to end things tonight?

"I, uh, wasn't sure how fancy you wanted to go tonight." He pulled into the parking lot of the waterfront restaurant. "I've never been here before, but I hear the food is excellent, and—"

"It's perfect," she assured him, and it was. The Northwest-casual restaurant had received top-notch reviews, and its position on a wharf just down from the ferry terminal promised outstanding views. "I'm impressed that you got reservations on such short notice."

"How impressed?" He waggled his eyebrows at her, and she couldn't help laughing. Just like that, the strain she'd been carrying all day dissipated. No matter how little time they had left, she was grateful to be spending it with the man she loved.

And no matter how much she wanted to deny it, she did love him. Maybe she had all along. In any case, she knew now that she had no choice but to tell him how she felt. If she'd learned anything during their time together, it was that wild women didn't weenie out of the hard things. It might be easier to leave the truth unsaid, but she'd never know if it could be more.

And if he didn't feel the same, well, at least she didn't have to worry about running into him everywhere.

The hostess led them through the crowded restaurant to the deck, where a table for two awaited them. A crisp white tablecloth fluttered gently in the breeze off the water, while a hurricane lamp cast a soft glow. A bottle of champagne chilled in an ice bucket between their chairs.

"Wow," she breathed. "Very, very impressed."

He grinned at her. "I'll keep that in mind later tonight," he said. Taking the menu from the hostess, he glanced out at the Sound. "I don't think I could ever get tired of that view."

"It is gorgeous, isn't it?" The setting sun cast red and orange patterns on the choppy water, sparking off the wake of a distant ferryboat. Sailboats traveled across the wide water, and a cruise ship bound for Canada sat in state on a neighboring pier. Across the Sound, the Olympic Mountains rose up from the waterline, a few patches of snow still visible even in the height of summer.

"Mmm-hmm," he said, but he was looking at her. Unable to hide a blush, even after two weeks of increasingly outrageous compliments, she just ducked her head and smiled.

Tonight. She had to tell him tonight. Without that, tomorrow would be nothing but gray.

ಸಂಞ

Cade Gallagher did not toy with his food.

He ate. He enjoyed. When he was done, he was done—take-the-plate-away, I-don't-need-it-anymore done.

So why in the world was he tracing patterns in the remnants of his garlic mashed potatoes?

Over the course of their meal, the sun had steadily slipped beneath the horizon, until the view had disappeared in velvet blackness. Lights winked across the dark water, indicating neighborhoods and offices, even the running lights on boats heading back to shore. The flame of the hurricane lamp on their table guttered in the brisk breeze.

As if on cue, Mollie shivered. Immediately, he stood, shucking off his jacket and placing it on her shoulders.

"No." She tried to hand it back. "I don't want you to get cold."

"I'm fine." If anything, he was overheated, and the cool night air would be a welcome change. Returning to his seat, he enjoyed the sight of the woman he loved wrapped in his jacket.

By the end of the evening, it would carry her scent, a sweet floral he could pick out anywhere now, a soft smell that reminded him of her. He'd probably never wash the stupid thing again.

Hopefully, it wouldn't be the only reminder he had of her.

"What time does your flight leave?" Her eyes were downcast, a slight strain visible at the edges. Her voice, trying so hard to be casual, betrayed a hint of emotion. Please, please let her be as affected as he was...

"Early. The shuttle is picking me up at five-thirty." He hated the thought of leaving, hated the idea of being apart from her, but the job had been set long before he knew how much he wanted to stay.

She waved a hand in the air. "Cancel it."

For a minute, his heart sped up. Did she want him to stay?

"I'll take you to the airport."

Oh. He settled back in his chair, hoping he hadn't betrayed his emotions just yet.

"I can't ask you to get up that early," he said.

"I volunteered." A small smile curved her lips. "Besides, I'm hoping I'll still be up by then."

His body leapt to attention at the innuendo. "Well, in that case..."

They both laughed, the ease of their relationship evident.

At least to him. And they did have a relationship, dammit! It was not just a hot and heavy, time-limited affair. He wouldn't let it be minimized like that anymore, by either of them.

"If you're sure you don't mind," he said, gratified when she shook her head vehemently.

"I insist." She sat back in her chair. "Especially after all you've done for me these past two weeks."

Not that again. Cade winced, hating the reminder of what she had wanted out of their time together. "Mollie..."

"No, let me finish." She leaned over the side of her chair and grabbed her purse, dropping it casually into her lap. Rummaging around in the interior, she pulled out a neatly folded piece of paper and waved it triumphantly. "I knew it was in here somewhere."

Cade eyed it warily. "Should I even ask?"

Mollie stuck out her tongue at him, momentarily diverting his attention to other, more carnal ideas. What that woman could do with her tongue... He shook his head, fiercely reminding himself that he had to stay focused.

"Hush. I didn't want to forget anything." She shook out the paper and cleared her throat. Glancing over the top of the paper, she eyed him somberly, looking for all the world like a librarian.

A hot, sexy, take-her-on-the-table-now librarian.

Focus! Dammit, focus!

"So here's my list of what I'm thankful for. One. You rescued me from that visit to Hell masquerading as a bachelor party." She smiled at him, eyes softening. "I can't imagine a better outcome to a horrible evening."

Cade coughed. "I'd have to agree with you there. But I still want to lodge a protest. This is not necessary."

"Protest noted and ignored." She looked at her list again. "Two. You introduced me to someone I'd wanted to get to know for a very, very long time." At his quizzical look, she clarified, "Myself. I'd been stifled by that good-girl mentality for so long, I didn't know who I really was. Now I feel like me, only better."

Cade shook his head again, but Mollie held up her hand.

"Three." Her voice shook a little. "You gave me a chance to find out what it really means to love someone. And even if I never get to see you again, I'll cherish that." Eyes fixed firmly on the tabletop, she folded up the paper with shaking hands and stuffed it back in her purse.

"Mollie." He reached over and lifted her chin, smiling inside at the way her gaze skittered away from him before turning back, almost defiantly.

"I know I said I wanted a no-strings affair. I know it's not fair to change the rules on you so late in the game, especially since you're leaving in the morning and heaven knows when you'll be back again, if ever. And I know I don't have any right to place a claim on you. But I do love you, Cade. And I didn't want you to leave without telling you the truth."

"I see." Cade took her hand in his, stroking the palm with his thumb. "Mollie, I—"

"Wait." She held up her free hand in a "stop" gesture. "Please don't try to let me down easy. If I hear the 'can't we just be friends' speech I think I'll crawl under the table and stay there. So just say what you're going to say. I can take it."

The wobble in her chin belied her brave words, but Cade nodded seriously anyway. "Actually, I was going to say it's about time for dessert."

She frowned at him. "Dessert?"

He turned, motioning to the waitress, who disappeared back into the main restaurant. "I ordered something in advance. I hope you don't mind."

"Uh, no," she said, brow furrowed.

"Great," he said easily, leaning back, hand still holding hers. "I think you'll enjoy it."

ഌൟ

Was the man insane?

She'd just declared her undying love, and all he could think about was dessert?

Mollie took a deep breath, trying to still the butterflies currently on combat maneuvers in her stomach. She'd worked up every ounce of nerve to tell him how she felt, and evidently he was too distracted by the thought of a sugar fix to respond.

Or maybe this *was* his response, she thought despondently. He didn't want to be cruel, and since she'd told him not to let her down easily, the only response he had left was to ignore the whole situation.

A disturbance at the doorway to the main restaurant drew her attention. Their waitress was directing two young men through the open doors, clearing the way for them. They were guiding a large wheeled cart between them.

"What on earth?" The cart drew closer, and Mollie could see what was on top of it. It was a three-layer, fully decorated cake.

To be specific, a wedding cake.

She looked around. Was there a reception being held here tonight? She hadn't seen a bridal couple, but that didn't mean...

Abruptly, the rumbling of the wheels on the cart stopped, and Cade rose to his feet. "Thanks." He handed some bills to the waitress, who split the tip with the young men. Smiling, the three walked back into the restaurant.

"Cade."

He turned around, a smile fighting its way onto his face. "Yes?"

"That's a wedding cake."

Cade nodded. "Yes, it is."

Mollie waited, but when he didn't elaborate, she tried again. "They brought us an entire wedding cake."

"Yes, they did."

"Why?"

Cade rounded the table and pulled her to her feet, wrapping his arms around her. "It seemed appropriate. After all, it was a wedding cake that brought us together."

She grimaced. "Don't remind me."

"Hey." He tipped her chin up and kissed her, long moments of urgency and fire until she sagged against him, all protest gone. "I don't care how we originally hooked up. All that matters is that we're together now."

"Cade..."

He shushed her with a brief, hard kiss to the lips. "This is my very inarticulate way of telling you that, though the sight of you popping out of that cake was my best fantasy come to life, *this* is the only cake I'll ever need with you."

She looked at him, unable to form a single word, until he sighed and smoothed the hair away from her face.

"Take a look at the top of the cake, Mollie, and put me out of my misery, okay?"

Confused and more than a little nervous, she stepped away from the warmth of his embrace and walked over to the cake. Instead of the traditional bride and groom on top, there was a spun-sugar jewelry box, propped open. Inside was a diamond ring.

"I..." Tears filled her eyes, and she blinked furiously, trying to clear them away. "I don't know what to say."

Cade coughed once. "I'd sort of hoped you might say yes." When she didn't respond immediately, he rushed on. "I know you just got out of a bad relationship, so I'll understand if you want to wait a while before taking a step like this. Just—just think about it, okay? I have to do this job in Dallas, but after that I'm planning to move back to town. Permanently."

"You're coming back?" She turned back to him, heart swelling at the sight of Cade standing there, a little uncertain, a lot hopeful.

"If there's something to come back to." He reached out and lifted one curl, tucking it behind her ear. "What do you say?"

In answer, she walked closer to the cake and carefully plucked the ring out of the candy holder. Eyes fixed on his, she slowly placed it on her finger.

"I don't have to wait," she said softly. "Hurry home."

She had just enough time to watch his face light up with joy before he pulled her into his arms, crushing his lips to hers as his hands stroked her back. They kissed hungrily, deeply, until the sound of clapping reminded them that they were, after all, in a public place. Pulling back, Mollie glanced around and then hid her face in Cade's shoulder. Half the restaurant had crowded to the open doorway to watch, and had burst into applause.

Turning her into the curve of his arm, he waved cheerfully at the gathered crowd and whispered in her ear, "Take a bow, wild woman."

She laughed at that, and waved to everyone as well. Then he steered her to the railing of the deck and turned their backs to the crowd.

"I hate leaving you." He pressed a kiss to the top of her head.

Smiling up at him, she squeezed him around the waist. "I don't mind."

"What?" He looked at her askance.

"It's only for a short time. That's what they invented phones for." She grinned evilly. "And I've never tried phone sex before."

"Okay, I can see the benefits," he said with a laugh.

"Besides," she said, pulling him down for another melt-your-socks-off kiss, "I know that at the end of it all, you'll be coming home. To me."

"Always." He lifted her into his arms. "Forever. Because home, for me, is where you are."

"Ditto." She snuggled in as he carried her off the deck, through the restaurant, and to the car.

Halfway through the main restaurant, they passed their waitress. She was carrying a stack of dessert plates and a knife. "Did you still want me to give everyone in the restaurant a piece of cake?"

"Absolutely," Cade said with a smile.

"But what about you?"

"Do you need a piece?" he asked Mollie, who shook her head.

"We'll have the real thing soon enough," she said with a smile, then waved to the waitress as Cade carried her out the door.

They were in a very, very big hurry to get home.

Strip Tease

Dedication

To Dad.

Thanks for always encouraging me to follow my dreams.

And thanks for being such a fine massage therapist—professional, dedicated, and capable. You're a true role model. I love you!

Chapter One

Caroline Richards was trapped in the eighties.

A bad music, big hair, completely tacky version of the eighties.

She sighed and stirred her over-watered drink, wishing she were anywhere but here. Mollie had a lot to answer for.

Of course, if Mollie knew what she was up to, she'd probably bust a blood vessel.

But she couldn't throw a proper bachelorette party without a stripper, could she?

"Hey, baby." A raspy voice interrupted her thoughts. She turned to find a man with Farrah Fawcett hair, a beer belly, a bow tie and what amounted to a Speedo standing at her table. "You ready for another screaming orgasm?"

She blinked twice, then looked down at her drink. Oh, yeah. "No, thanks," she replied. Why try another? It hadn't lived up to its name the first time around. More like a whimper.

He shrugged and headed back to the bar, leaving her alone again.

For a Friday night, the place was pretty dead. A group of five women whooped it up a few tables over, passing around some physically impossible sex toys and ignoring the man gyrating on stage only a few feet away.

Caroline didn't blame them. It was painfully obvious the guy was lacking in the toy department himself, and his dancing—to use the term loosely—reminded her of a toddler learning the Macarena. The music built to a crescendo, and he whipped the cowboy hat off his head, flinging it into the air.

She lunged sideways, barely missing being smacked in the face with the limp, battered felt hat. The song ended and he yee-hawed himself offstage, leaving his hat as a memento no one seemed inclined to collect.

One more. She'd stay for one more, and then she was out of there. Best friend or no best friend, she was fast reaching her tolerance level for talentless guys taking their clothes off.

She could get that on a blind date any day of the week.

Caroline snorted. Maybe that was why she hadn't dated in almost a year.

She sighed, wondering if she could talk Mollie's fiancé into being the stripper at the bachelorette party. God knows he'd look better than any of the losers she'd seen this evening.

On second thought, better not. Mollie was a terrific friend, generous and thoughtful, but she'd probably draw the line at letting her friends ogle Cade while he took his clothes off.

Caroline sighed again, taking another sip of her watery drink. Maybe she should give up now, head home and put in the DVD of *Pride and Prejudice* for the umpteenth time. She felt stupid and awkward sitting alone in this creepy place, and she obviously wasn't finding what she was looking for here.

Not for the first time, she wished she had come here with a friend. At least with a partner-in-crime she'd have someone to crack jokes with, instead of feeling so conspicuous. Pathetic. Alone.

But other than Mollie, she didn't have any close friends, certainly no one she'd feel comfortable asking to join her at

Seattle's newest—and only—strip club for women. And she couldn't ask Mollie to help her pick out a stripper for her own bachelorette party, for obvious reasons.

Well, tonight had been a massive waste of time. She bent over and reached for her purse, which had migrated under the table during the evening. Her fingers brushed the straps, but it was beyond her reach. Cursing under her breath, she twisted underneath the tabletop and stretched a little further.

Suddenly, music blasted from the ancient sound system, startling Caroline and making her jump, smacking her head against the underside of the table. Tossing out a few more curse words for variety, she wriggled out from under the table, rubbing her head.

Then she stopped, riveted on the stage in front of her. She was tempted to pinch herself, just to make sure she wasn't fantasizing the man who'd appeared onstage.

And oh, what a fantasy he was! The faux police uniform looked spray-painted on, showcasing a drool-worthy body. His arms flexed and bunched as he released each button on his tight shirt one by one. It fell open to reveal a wide, muscled chest, with the perfect amount of hair—not too fuzzy, not nonexistent—and sleek, lightly tanned skin that begged to be touched.

He stripped off the shirt, tossing it away as he began to work on the fly of his pants. Caroline swallowed, her mouth suddenly dry, as she noticed that the rest of him seemed as large as what had already been revealed.

The music throbbed in the air around her, the theme from a popular police show adding a strong drumbeat as he stripped down to a well-filled-out, and extremely small, brief.

Caroline was gripped by a sudden urge to scream for him to take it all off, even though she knew this was as far as he was going to go. The other strippers had all stopped at their skivvies, which hadn't bothered her a bit.

Not until now.

Now, she would buy a round of screaming orgasms for the whole room if she got to see Officer Friendly do the full monty.

The music ground to a halt and the lights dimmed, announcing the end of the act. She sat back, disappointed, as he flashed a grin but nothing else while he made his way offstage.

She glanced around, not surprised to find the few other women in the club just as enthralled as she was in the latest act. The partiers had even abandoned their investigation of the X-rated gifts piling the table and were chanting for his return.

Until that moment, Caroline would have given Strippendale's another three months in business, if that. There was probably a very good reason the club had no competitors, because really, how much of a market was there for a women-only strip club? The audience tonight had been pathetically small. But with a man like that showing off his assets, the club might stand a fighting chance.

Another song started playing, and Caroline shook off her musings. This guy, whoever he was, would be perfect for Mollie's bachelorette party. And she'd better get backstage and find out if he was available before she lost her chance—and her nerve.

℘ↄα

Tony DiMarco loved his job.

Which was a good thing, because if he had to strip for a living, he figured he'd just kill himself and avoid the agony.

But drastic situations called for drastic measures, and working undercover at Strippendale's certainly fit the vice squad's definition of drastic.

Bump and grind music filtered through the flimsy walls of what passed for a dressing room. The other guys, thank God, had moved to the bar after their sets so he had the place to himself for at least a little while. Skimming off the embarrassingly tight briefs, he hustled into his after-strip outfit—boxers, well-worn jeans and a University of Washington sweatshirt. He sighed in relief, settling into the single folding chair to decompress for a few moments before all hell broke loose.

The department had been investigating Strippendale's for months now, but when details were slow in appearing, Captain Matthews had decided that they would do much better with someone on the inside.

He'd drawn the short end of the stick. See if he ever offered to bring coffee for the team again. Two minutes out of the briefing room and he'd been "volunteered".

Tony sighed, scrubbing a hand through his hair in frustration. As usual, the captain had been right. He'd learned more in the two weeks he'd been working here than the entire team had dug up in the three months prior.

His first night, his suspicions that something didn't add up about Strippendale's had been confirmed. The place had been dead, only a few pathetic souls scattered throughout the room. It didn't make sense, especially for a weekend night, but there had been barely enough customers to pay the electrical bill, let alone generate the kind of revenue that was passing through the place on a regular basis.

It had to be a front for something.

Within three days, he'd been offered drugs. Four, and he'd been the lookout for a transaction. And by the end of his first week there, he'd been invited to join the after-hours club.

Helloooo, prostitution ring.

He'd managed to walk the tightrope between vague interest and actual participation all week, long enough to gather the hard evidence he needed to set up the bust.

Tonight, the place was going down.

And, thank God, his strip career was ending as well.

It had been humiliating enough to shed his clothes for an audience for the past two weeks. Tonight, however, had been a new level of hell. Any good bust required fellow officers to stake out the location—but did every one of his female colleagues have to attend the show?

Oh, the things he did to make the world safe for democracy.

A staccato rap on the door put him on alert. He wasn't expecting a contact until the bust went down. The last thing he needed was to blow his cover too soon.

"Come in." He sat back in the folding chair. The door opened, and she walked in.

It was the customer. Or rather, The Customer. The one he'd noticed right off, even over the wince-inducing shock of seeing his colleagues in the audience. Of all the places he might expect to see a woman like this, a sleazy strip club was pretty much last on his list.

The first thing he'd noticed about her was her hair. Flame red, with a hint of curl, it swooped around her shoulders like that cartoon babe from Roger Rabbit, all sexy and sort of retro. A half-smile curved full red lips. And her body—have mercy.

What the hell was she doing at Strippendale's?

Strip Tease

"Can I help you?" He prayed the rickety chair wouldn't collapse and dump him on his ass.

"Yeah," she said, and licked her bottom lip. Shit, who needed a collapsing chair? That little nervous gesture almost dropped him to the floor. "I, uh, really liked your..." She waved her hand around. "Uh, your show."

Hell. If the guys down at the station knew he was getting groupies, he'd never live it down. Then again, a groupie who looked like a long tall shot of sex might not be such a bad thing, either. "Thanks," he drawled.

"I'm Caroline," She held out her hand.

He shook it, trying not to react to the softness of her skin contrasting with the firmness of her grip. "Tony," he replied, motioning her to sit.

Too late, he remembered that he had the only chair, but before he could offer it to her, she had perched on the counter in front of the mirror. Her skirt hiked up, giving him a splendid view of her long, slim legs.

Why, why, *why* did he have to meet her here?

And why tonight, fifteen minutes before the operation was shut down for good?

"And I, uh, was wondering..." This time, she bit that poor abused lower lip. He wanted to take it home and lavish it with loving care. Oh, the things he could do with that lip...

Okay, man, focus. "Wondering what?"

She fiddled with her purse, then took a deep breath. "I was wondering if you were available."

Hallelujah!

"You know, outside the club." She looked him straight in the eye for the first time tonight. "How much do you charge?"

Damn.

101

Just like that, his private fantasy turned into another nail in Strippendale's coffin.

"I really liked you," she continued. "So I was wondering, do I have to clear this with someone, or do you work privately?"

This had to be the first time she'd done this. Otherwise, she'd know that management handled all the gigolo action.

Just her bad luck she decided to take a walk on the sleazy side tonight.

He sighed inwardly, wishing he had met her somewhere else, under very different circumstances. He didn't understand why the hell someone who looked like her felt the need to pay for sex.

"What are you willing to pay?" If she took the bait, he'd have no choice but to haul her in with the rest.

"I don't know." She colored a little, an interesting contrast with her gorgeous hair. "I've never done this before. Is two hundred enough?"

"Sounds about right." He stood up. Even in her high-heeled shoes, she only came up to his shoulder. Brushing past her, he pushed the door all the way open. "What do you say we head back into the club and finish our negotiations there?"

She smiled at him, and it was like a fist to the gut. Why did she have to be so sexy, so enticing, so—sweet? Her smile had none of the hard-edged cynicism he had grown used to over ten years of working vice.

But if he'd learned anything during those years, it was never to trust appearances.

He held the door for her, taking the opportunity to check out her assets as she walked past him into the hallway. Then he escorted her out of the backstage area—and straight into hell.

ℰℴℛ

What the hell?

Caroline stopped at the entryway into the club, staring around in confusion. When she'd slipped backstage, everything had been calm, almost comatose, especially since the stripper who had followed Tony had been the poster child for anticlimactic.

Now, the entire room was in chaos. People were shouting, tables knocked over, drinks spilled across the floor. A uniformed police officer stood in the doorway yelling orders through a megaphone that no one was listening to. One of the bachelorette party attendees was bent over the funky-haired waiter, her knee in the small of his back, cuffing his hands behind him. Another was lining up the dancers against the far wall, holding a gun on them.

A gun! Caroline backed away, trying to escape the madhouse in front of her. There had to be a back exit somewhere around here...

She made it a couple of steps before she ran into a solid object. A warm, well-muscled, breathing object. "Where are you going?" Tony gripped her upper arms.

Any other time, she would have focused on how good it felt to have his hands on her. Right now, though, she only wanted to escape. "We have to get out of here. The whole place has gone crazy." She turned just enough to see his profile. "I think some people are getting arrested."

She couldn't get caught up in this. It was tough enough being a massage therapist, what with all the assumptions about the profession. If news got out that she'd visited a strip club—

especially one where illegal activities were evidently happening—it could destroy her career and her reputation.

"This is a bust," Tony said in her ear, his hands sliding down her arms.

"I know," she hissed back. "I can't be found here. Is there a back door or something?"

"Yes," he said, his fingers circling her wrists. "But you won't be using it."

Too late, she realized he was snapping something around her wrists. "What are you doing?" She struggled, but the restraints were metal and unyielding.

"You have the right to remain silent," he answered. Grasping her by the elbow, he pulled her into the main room. "Everything you say can and will be used against you in a court of law."

"You're arresting me?" Caroline knew she was shrieking, but it wasn't as if anyone could hear her besides the stripper-slash-cop dragging her into the fray. "What for?"

"Solicitation." He turned her around so she was lined up with the rest of the criminals. Criminals!

"Solic—" She gaped at him. "You thought I was trying to pay you for *sex*?"

Silence descended on the room, heads swiveling her direction.

"You have the right to an attorney," Tony continued, unaffected by her outburst.

"I was trying to hire a stripper for a friend's bachelorette party, you moron," she yelled, too angry to care that they were the center of attention.

"Let's get everyone down to headquarters and sort this out," a female cop said, placing her hand on Tony's shoulder. Her lips twitched, as if she were trying to hold back a grin. "Nice show, by the way. I don't blame her for wanting to see you strip again, whatever the circumstances."

"Stuff it, Phillips," he replied, his gaze focused on Caroline.

"You probably do." Caroline looked at his groin contemptuously. "And after I sue you for false arrest, you'd better believe I never want to see you—in or out of your clothes—again."

Chapter Two

"You're calling me from *jail?*"

Caroline pulled the phone away from her ear. She winced as Mollie's voice rose several octaves. "Do I have to repeat myself? It was hard enough to say the first time."

She held the receiver by her fingertips, creeped out by the nasty thing. Everything in the industrial green holding area seemed covered by a layer of dirt and some unidentifiable sticky stuff. Her shoes stuck to the floor, and when she stood up from the bench to make her phone call, her skirt had tried to stay behind.

"Give me the address," Mollie demanded, crinkling sounds carrying over the phone line. "I've got paper and pen."

Caroline repeated the location and threw in some directions for good measure. She'd been here before, to pay a parking fine, but never on this side of the building.

She never wanted to be here again.

"Can you tell me what's going on?" Mollie's voice held no censure, only caring concern. To her horror, Caroline felt her eyes well with tears.

Angrily, she swiped them away. "I'll fill you in on all the gory details once you get here," she said. "Just—just hurry, okay?"

Mollie said goodbye and hung up, leaving Caroline to wait. Around her, women sat on the benches, some obviously high, others trying to sleep sitting up, their heads against the peeling walls.

Please, please hurry, Mollie.

She stood in the center of the holding cell, arms wrapped around her waist. This had to be the worst night of her entire life.

Thanks to Mr. "Oops, I really *am* a cop" Tony the Stripper. God, she didn't even know his last name.

Not that she wanted to know it.

No, she wanted nothing to do with the man. Ever again.

The hell of it was, he'd seemed like a nice guy. He hadn't laughed at her, even when she fumbled around trying to hire him for Mollie's party. His handshake had been firm and warm, no limp fish or beer-can-crushing grip. And he'd looked her in the eyes when she talked.

Oh, she'd caught the look, the almost involuntary eye dip to chest level when they'd first started talking. She'd been a 38D since her sophomore year of high school, and had long since grown immune to the double takes. But when men talked to her chest, well, it was beyond annoying.

What, did they expect her breasts to start talking back?

But after that initial glance, Tony No-Last-Name had kept his eyes locked on hers, rather than roaming her curves. And she'd appreciated that.

At least until he'd slapped the cuffs on her and ruined her life.

A woman in uniform poked her head in the door and looked around. "Caroline Richards?"

Caroline nodded and followed her out of the room. On the other side of the door, it was a bit cleaner, smelling of industrial-strength antiseptic. She sucked in a deep lungful, painfully relieved to be out of the holding cell. The woman led her to a counter, where she retrieved a plastic bag filled with Caroline's belongings.

"Thank you," she mumbled, eyes fixed on the bag.

"You've been officially cleared of all charges." The officer motioned to the doorway. "Sorry for the inconvenience."

"Inconvenience?" Caroline stared at her with astonishment. She'd been cuffed, arrested, driven to the station in the back of a police car—with sirens blaring!—and left in lock-up for hours while they sorted out the situation. Worse than that, though, was the news crew that had somehow sniffed out the bust in advance and had captured her humiliation on camera. Tony had tried to shield her face from the cameras as they left the building, but she knew it had been no use. The damage was done, and no amount of lame half-assed apologies would make up for that.

"Are you all right?" Mollie rushed through the swinging doors, eyes filled with concern. She wrapped an arm around Caroline's shoulders and steered her out of the room. "What happened?"

Caroline blinked as her eyes adjusted to the darkness outside the building. She stood on the steps for a minute, getting her bearings, while Mollie waited patiently. She noticed that Mollie had thrown on a sweatshirt over her flannel pajamas, not bothering to get dressed before coming to her rescue.

She hated the fact that she even needed to be rescued. She could take care of herself, thank you very much. But in this case, she had little choice.

"Let's get out of here, grab a mocha and some Oreos, and I'll tell you the whole sordid story." Maybe with some caffeine and chocolate in her system she could resist the urge to put her head on Mollie's shoulder and cry.

Mollie gave her another squeeze and let go, giving her the space she needed.

It had started to rain since she'd been inside, and she pulled her coat around her in an attempt to stay dry. She started down the steps, dodging the puddle that had gathered right in the center of the old concrete.

She could hear footsteps behind them, coming closer as they reached the sidewalk. A tap on the shoulder made her turn.

Wouldn't you know it. Officer Friendly.

"Ms. Richards, I wanted to offer a personal apology before you left," he said, eyes intent on hers. "Upon reviewing our conversation, I realized that your rendition of events was accurate and I jumped to conclusions. I'm sorry I accused you of solicitation."

Caroline ignored Mollie's reaction, which was somewhere between a gasp and a smothered laugh. "You didn't just accuse me of trying to pay you for sex. You arrested me for it!"

"That's my job," he argued. "I was in the middle of an investigation of a prostitution ring. You were in the wrong place at the wrong time, saying the wrong thing. It was nothing personal."

"Tell that to my clients who probably saw me on the eleven o'clock news." She waved her hand in a tired gesture. "Never mind. Apology accepted."

A muscle in his jaw worked, but he was interrupted by a shout from the doorway of the building. "Hey, DiMarco!" A woman stood in the doorway, silhouetted by the fluorescent lighting inside. Caroline recognized her as one of the other cops from the bust. "Get your ass in here and help me with this paperwork!"

"In a minute," he shouted back, then turned to Caroline again. "You said clients. Is there going to be a problem with—"

The other cop took the steps two at a time, reaching the group at the bottom of the stairs. "Hey, you're the chick from the strip club," she said. "Tony really fucked that one up, huh?"

"Yes, I did, and thank you for pointing that out," he growled, while Mollie stared pointedly at Caroline.

Strip club? Mollie mouthed.

Caroline pretended not to notice. "It's fine. In fact, I'd prefer to forget this ever happened."

The other cop nodded. "I understand. Tony here hasn't figured out he can't fix everything. He's the Pollyanna of the department." With a smile, she elbowed him in the side. "Come on, Mr. Fix-It. Time to fix the paperwork disaster from this lovely event."

Tony looked like he wanted to argue, but in the end he merely nodded and stepped aside. "Good night," he said. He climbed the steps and pulled open the door to the station, holding it for his fellow officer.

Caroline watched him leave, wishing she'd never gone to that damn strip club, wishing she'd met him under different circumstances, wishing she was anywhere but the steps of the police station in the rain, looking at the first man she'd been attracted to in ages disappear inside the doors.

"Who the hell was that?" Mollie was watching him as well, her eyes round.

Caroline sighed, shoving a hand through her tangled hair. The combination of smoke from the club, humidity in the holding cell, and misting rain had conspired to turn her into a total frizz ball. "The guy who arrested me." Now where the hell was Mollie's lime green Bug?

Mollie grabbed her arm and steered her down the street to the parking lot. "I gathered that much. Did he say you tried to pay him for sex?"

"Yes, that's what he thought, no, I wasn't, and anyway the charges were dropped."

"Then what were you trying to do?"

Caroline shrugged her shoulders and mumbled, "Hire a stripper for your bachelorette party."

Mollie smacked her on the arm. "Serves you right for ignoring me," she said. "After the fiasco with you-know-who's bachelor party, you should know the idea of a stripper gives me the willies. Male or female."

"I thought you deserved one last hurrah before you get married." Caroline sidestepped the puddle in front of her.

"Maybe if I was still getting married to the creep. But I'm marrying Cade. He's all the man I'll ever need."

Caroline waited as Mollie unlocked the passenger door, then hurried over to the driver's side. Sliding into the car, she thought about what Mollie had said. She couldn't imagine ever being that wrapped up in another person.

When she looked at Cade and Mollie together, though, sometimes she felt a little twinge at how well they complemented each other.

"I do have to say you have good taste," Mollie commented as she started up the car.

Caroline shook her head and tried to focus back on the conversation. "Hmmm?"

"That guy back there. The stripper-cop-person you got tangled up with tonight. He was a total hottie." Mollie grinned at Caroline. "Not as gorgeous as Cade, but still cute."

"You should have seen him strip." She smiled back. "He set the place on fire."

Unwanted, an image popped into her head, the same one that had been tormenting her ever since she'd arrived at this place. Colored lights swirled over Tony's sleek skin as he peeled away his shirt, one button at a time.

"I wonder if he's single." Mollie laughed at Caroline's outraged look. "For you, doofus. Anyone can tell you've got a bit of a crush on the man."

Caroline rolled her eyes. "The man arrested me and had me thrown in jail," she reminded her. "That's a bit of an issue to work past."

"Might be worth it, though," Mollie said, but Caroline just shook her head.

She should be nursing a monster-sized grudge right now, ready to sue his ass for false arrest and whatever else she could get to stick, anything to salvage her reputation and her fledgling career in massage therapy. Instead, she was sitting there, wondering if Mollie was right.

Because even after all that had happened, he was still the first man in forever who had looked her in the eye.

ಬಂಛ

Well, he'd totally blown that one.

Big time.

Tony shook his head and dropped into his desk chair with a heavy sigh. His desktop was, as usual, covered with paperwork. Captain Matthews bitched about it on a regular basis, enough to guilt him into shuffling the papers around so it looked tidier.

Like most cops, he suspected that he'd be more likely to die by paperwork than in the line of duty.

Right on top was the beginning of his report for tonight's bust, a mishmash of details he needed to organize before sending it on up the chain of command. And thanks to his rookielike eagerness to catch the bad guys, he had to include his massive leap-to-conclusions about Caroline Richards.

Closing his eyes, he scrubbed one hand through his tousled hair. He'd been so sure she was propositioning him, and after spending two weeks in the sleazy underground of Strippendale's, who could blame him?

But after reviewing their actual conversation—and discussing it with Phillips, who despite her teasing was the person he trusted most on the squad—he admitted that she'd never asked for sex. She liked his act and wanted to hire him. To strip.

It was his own bias that put the solicitation angle on their discussion.

Once he'd realized that, he couldn't get the charges dropped fast enough. The first woman he'd been attracted to in way too long, and he'd put her in jail. *Smooth move, slick.*

At least she hadn't opened a can of whoop-ass on him outside just now. He'd apologized, not that it was enough for what she'd been through, but he hadn't been able to get beyond "sorry".

Maybe he could track her down tomorrow or the next day, ask her out for coffee or something, see if the attraction was still a mutual thing.

Because before he'd blown everything to hell with that whole "you have the right to remain silent" crap, he knew she'd been interested in him, too. Hell, she'd liked him enough to ask him to take his clothes off again, even if it was for a bachelorette party. Maybe she'd be open to a private showing, off the clock, of course.

And maybe she'd want to return the favor.

He rolled his eyes. She'd already told him that she wanted to see him again—naked or not—like she wanted a hole in the head.

Still, like Phillips said, he was a born optimist. Might as well give it a good old college try.

⊗⊘

Caroline hung up the phone, scratching another name off her appointment sheet. Mrs. Knight had been very apologetic, so sorry that she had a conflict and wouldn't be able to make her massage this week. She might not be able to make next week's, either.

Conflict, my ass. Chalk another one up to the Great Strip Club Massacre.

She stared at the scribbled-out mess that used to be her appointment sheet, until her eyes started to cross and the lines swam together. She'd lost roughly two-thirds of her clientele over the past three days, and the attrition was likely to continue.

Somehow, the fact that all charges had been dropped hadn't been considered newsworthy. The shot of her being stuffed into a squad car, though, handcuffs glinting in the glare of the cameras, had been the lead of every newscast for a day and a half after it happened.

What was that saying about any publicity being good publicity? Total crap.

Apparently, Seattleites got a little skittish about massage therapists who were arrested at sleazy strip joints.

Now, with one misstep, all of her hard work had been blown to hell.

She sighed again, tapping a pen on her desktop. With luck, she'd be able to make rent on her office this month. If she didn't lose any more clients. And if she only ate two meals a day.

She checked her watch, wishing it were almost five instead of almost noon. Maybe she should just head home early, instead of waiting for foot traffic to drop by. Her office was centrally located, but only rarely did she get new clients from drop-ins. Word of mouth and referrals were the best way she'd found to improve her client base.

Unfortunately, she doubted any word of mouth would be positive nowadays.

Caroline blew out a frustrated breath, then started gathering up her bag and some end-of-the-month paperwork. She could get started on them at home. Anything was better than sitting here in her empty massage office, trying to find something to keep her busy and her mind off the lack of clients.

The bell on her door chimed, announcing a visitor. Her noon appointment had already cancelled so she wasn't expecting anyone. Maybe it was a new client?

She shuddered, hoping it wasn't a sleazeball like the last two who'd decided her notorious arrest indicated she offered other services along with her deep tissue massage.

Caroline pasted a smile on her face and stood, ready to walk into the tiny entryway known affectionately as a lobby, when a not-entirely-unwelcome face appeared around her office doorway.

"Officer," she said, her stomach swooping and diving at the sight of the man she'd thought about far too much over the past three days. "Is there a problem?"

"Nice place you got here." He looked around with an appraising air. "I'm impressed."

"Gee, thanks." Somehow, the room seemed smaller, hotter, with him in it.

He flashed her a brief smile that dimpled one cheek and sent a shudder of heat roaming through her nervous system.

"Was there something in particular you wanted, Officer?"

"Please, call me Tony. I'm not here on official business."

"I don't even know your last name."

He stuffed one hand in his jeans pocket. "Sorry. It's DiMarco."

"Tony DiMarco." She ignored the little tremor of awareness that swept through her. "Is there something I can do for you, Officer DiMarco?"

"Tony."

"Tony." She raised one eyebrow, waiting for an explanation for his visit.

"I could use a backrub."

"Excuse me?"

"You're a massage therapist, right? My shoulders have been killing me. I need a good rubdown. Do you have any appointments available today?"

She pictured the scribbled-out appointment sheet and had to stifle a snort of laughter. "I might," she hedged.

"Great. Why don't you check your book and put me down? I've got the afternoon off, so I'm flexible."

Yeah, she knew that. She'd seen that trait in action, down at Strippendale's.

"I'm not sure if—"

"Come on. I could use a good massage."

"How do you know I'm good?"

His glance was full of promise. "I have a sense for this sort of thing."

This time, she really did snort. "Right. Look, Officer DiMarco, I appreciate your kindness, but there's no need."

"Tony. And no need for what?"

She waved a hand at the empty room. "Your sense of obligation. Yeah, my business is running rough these days, but it'll survive." She hoped. "You don't have to make an appointment to ease your guilt."

His brows drew together, making him look almost forbidding. "You think this is a pity thing? Please. I'd really have to force myself to suffer through a backrub." He pinned her with a glare, taking one step forward. "And what's this bullshit about guilt? I have nothing to feel guilty about. I was doing my job."

"Fine."

"Good."

Caroline glared back at him, furious that he'd spun up her temper yet again. At least they didn't have an audience this time.

"So do I get the massage or what?"

Caroline grabbed her appointment sheet off her desk and pretended to study it. "I can squeeze you in right now, since I don't have a client at noon." Or at one, or two, or pretty much the rest of the afternoon, but he didn't have to know that.

"Sounds good. How much do you charge?"

The question was a little too reminiscent of their exchange at the strip club, so instead of answering she slapped a brochure into his hand. "Services and rates are listed in here. Why don't you go into the massage room, strip to the waist, and get on the table underneath the sheet. I'll be with you in a few minutes."

Turning on her heel, she went back into her office and barely resisted slamming the door shut. There was no reason for her to be so irritated by this, but she was. Unfortunately, her bank account dictated that she take the job, whether it was a pity thing or not.

But her attitude needed a serious adjustment first. She needed to get over herself before starting this massage, or she wouldn't be up to her usual standards. She looked down, chagrined to see her hands were trembling a little bit.

And a tiny voice inside kept nagging that it was more about her attraction towards Tony DiMarco than any blow to her pride.

A click of the door informed her that Tony was in the massage room. She tried not to imagine him taking off his shirt, slipping under the cool sheet on her massage table. It had been foolhardy to agree to this massage in the first place, but it was done and she had to be a professional about it. Sighing, she pulled her hair back from her face and secured it in place with a scrunchy.

If only she didn't want to put her hands on him for other reasons, life would be so much easier.

৪১৫

He was in heaven. Tony sighed, rotating his shoulders as Caroline tidied up her supplies. "That was magnificent," he said, his voice muffled, which made sense considering he was facedown on a padded table.

"Thanks," she replied, her voice clipped and distant.

Tony eased into a seated position. "I'll definitely have to recommend you to the other guys on the force."

"Thanks," she said again. Her eyes remained fixed on the shelf, where she was organizing her oils and lotions. "I appreciate the vote of confidence." She snagged his shirt off the hanger and handed it to him, eyes still averted. "Go ahead and get dressed and I'll see you in the lobby." With a brief nod, she slipped out of the room.

Rolling his shoulders again, Tony shrugged into the shirt. His hands stilled on the buttons as he turned his head from side to side, enjoying the extra range of motion from his relaxed muscles. Why hadn't he done this before?

Because he didn't know any legitimate massage therapists, except for Caroline Richards, he admitted to himself, slipping into his shoes. His experience with masseuses had all been through his job, and establishments visited by vice cops tended to be low on massage and high on other illegal practices.

The ladies he'd busted in massage parlors had been there for one reason. Unfortunately, they also tended to give all massage therapists a bad name.

And parading Caroline Richards past the news cameras on the way to his cop car had probably cemented that idea in a lot of people's eyes.

Masseuse plus sleazy strip club equals bad reputation. And despite his protestations to Caroline, he did feel somewhat responsible for the fallout.

He'd been searching for a reason to see her again. The killer backrub was just a bonus.

He'd seen the appointment sheet on Caroline's desk when he came in, and realized right off that the scribbled-out paper was proof of the consequence of her arrest last weekend. His eagerness to bust the Strippendale's drug and prostitution ring had snared an innocent, and she was paying the price.

Well, getting a massage was definitely no hardship, and if it helped her out a bit, so much the better.

She was sitting at her desk when he came out of the massage room, and he handed over the fee with a smile. He reached out and snagged a handful of her cards from the stack on the edge of the desk. "I'll drop them by the station house," he said.

"Thank you," she replied, ripping a slip of paper out of her receipt book. "I hope your back feels better."

"Better than it has in years." He stretched his arms overhead. "It's amazing."

"Massage has a lot of health benefits. Studies show it improves muscle tone, increases range of motion, even lowers blood pressure and stress levels."

"Well, you definitely have the magic touch." He pocketed the receipt and smiled at her. "Same time next week?"

"Excuse me?"

"Consider me your newest regular. I'm telling you, those hands of yours are amazing."

To his amazement—and secret delight—she blushed at that. He hadn't been exaggerating, either. His back felt better than it had in years. Unfortunately, it also occurred to him how amazing those hands would feel on other parts of his body.

"Uh, okay." She flipped to next week's appointment sheet. "I guess I'll see you then." She checked her watch, a nervous gesture that Tony found oddly endearing. "Thanks for coming in," she said. "I should probably start getting ready for my next client, so…"

And with that, Tony knew his time with Caroline was coming to a swift end. "Have coffee with me," he said.

"Sorry," she replied, eyes still focused on her appointment book. "I can't."

He reached over and tapped the scribbled-out page. "Not to rub salt in your wounds, but you're obviously not busy for the rest of the day. Come on, it'll be my treat."

She sighed and looked directly in his eyes for the first time since he'd arrived at her office. "Officer DiMarco, I am a professional. I work very hard to keep my professional and personal lives separate. Any hint of impropriety can be devastating to a business such as mine." She eyed him closely. "As you so brilliantly deduced from my appointment calendar."

Ouch. "Point taken," he said. "But I doubt that an innocent coffee would cause that much damage."

She was wavering, he could tell; her eyes flicked almost involuntarily to the appointment sheet, then her watch.

"Tell you what," he said. "I'm heading down to the Starbucks on the corner. Meet me there in ten minutes or so, just to talk. As friends. Okay?"

She made a move with her head, could have been either a nod or a shake, but he didn't give her a chance to clarify. Instead, he smiled and slipped out the door.

In ten minutes, she'd either be there, or not. The time wasn't right to press her for more, even if he wanted to. But he sure hoped her answer would be yes.

Chapter Three

What the hell was she doing?

Caroline stopped in her tracks, ready to turn right around and go back to her office. Coffee with Tony DiMarco was a bad, bad idea.

She'd barely made it through the massage with her professionalism intact. It had been ages since she'd been that attracted to someone, and to have her hands on him, well, it was torture.

Sheer torture.

And now he'd sweet-talked her into meeting for coffee, just between friends? Yeah, right. She'd seen the look in his eyes. Innocent was not the word she'd use to describe it.

And deep down, she admitted that innocent was the last thing she wanted to be with him.

She'd wanted him since the moment she'd laid eyes on him, and much to her chagrin, that hadn't changed, even after the mess at Strippendale's. If anything, his nice-guy personality made him even more attractive in her eyes.

But it couldn't work, for so many reasons. She shouldn't be here.

It was too late, though. She could see him through the window, sitting at a table facing the street. He saw her, lifted his cup in greeting, and she knew there would be no escape. He knew it, too, if the wry smile on his face was any indication.

Darn it, she didn't want to be attracted to him. She should have told him in no uncertain terms that she wasn't interested in any kind of relationship with him, especially after he'd been the cause of so much turmoil in her life, starting with being thrown in jail. But the hard truth was, that would be a lie. She was interested. And she could tell he knew it, too.

Shaking her head at her own foolishness, she walked inside the coffee shop and ordered her drink. Tony stood, reaching for his wallet, but she waved him off. This wasn't a date, and she always paid for herself when having coffee with friends.

Or she would, if she had coffee-date friends. She and Mollie sometimes met up for a latte, but offhand she couldn't think of a single other person in her life that she could call up to meet for coffee or anything else.

And right now, that was almost more depressing than the state of her business.

She paid for her latte and stood at the counter, preferring to wait for her drink. Okay, maybe she was stalling a little, too. The barista tipped the industrial-style whipped cream container on end, swirling a perfect dollop on top of her drink. Immediately she flashed to an image of Tony stretched out on the tabletop, as bare as he'd been at the strip club, grinning up at her as she wielded the whipped cream dispenser over his gorgeous chest.

And slowly, slowly licked it off.

Oh, she had it bad.

He half-stood when she reached the table, his devilish smile igniting even more sparks inside her. "Glad you could make it." He set his cup on the table. "I hate to drink alone."

She sat down across from him. "Hitting the hard stuff already, huh?"

He nodded. "Double shot and extra whipped cream. Don't tell anyone."

He would have to bring up whipped cream, wouldn't he? Damn the man, anyway.

She took a sip of her latte, wincing as the hot liquid seared the inside of her mouth.

"Careful," he said. "I'd hate to see anything happen to that mouth of yours."

"Why?" Suspicious, she looked at him askance.

He smiled. "Never mess with perfection."

She lowered her gaze, aware that a slight blush was heating her cheeks. She'd never gotten used to accepting compliments, and Tony's were even harder to take because they seemed so sincere.

"So tell me about yourself," he said, leaning back in his chair.

"What do you want to know?"

Tony shrugged. "The usual. Where you're from, about your family. Why massage."

Caroline latched onto the easy question. "I became a massage therapist because of my grandmother." Even rotating her shoulders didn't do much to help her relax. She was carrying a boatload of tension, some of it sexual, and knew if she didn't loosen her muscles she'd pay for it the next day.

His eyes brightened. "That sounds like an interesting story."

Caroline looked down at her hands. What was it about him that got her talking about things she never shared? For some reason, though, she felt safe with him. As if he were interested in her for *her*, and not just because of how she looked. "She had cancer pretty bad, the last year of her life. And one of the only things that helped was massage. It relaxed her, took away a lot of the pain. I decided to go back to school and get my license, start my own practice."

"What did you do before that?"

Caroline shrugged. "Little of this, little of that. I was a waitress for a while, worked in a bookstore. No big career to dump for the alternative healthcare field. Besides," she said with a shaky laugh, "I've always been told I'm good with my hands."

The look he gave her was heated and full of promise. "I can agree with that."

Her thighs clenched at the thought of putting her hands on him again—this time as a lover.

No two ways about it—she wanted him. And she hadn't wanted anyone in a long, long time.

"So you and your grandma were close," he said, as if it were a foregone conclusion.

Of course, he was a cop. They were trained to read situations. Too bad his reading was a little off.

She nodded, dipping her head down so he couldn't see her expression. "I lived with her from junior high on."

"Really?" Surprise tinged his voice. "Why's that?"

Caroline shrugged. "The usual. Didn't get along with my mom, blah blah blah." She propped her elbows on the tabletop and rested her chin on her hands. "So tell me about your family."

He raised an eyebrow, as if informing her that he saw right through her diversionary tactic, but thankfully he didn't call her on it. "Big, loud, Italian. I've got four brothers and two sisters, six nieces and nephews, and more aunts and uncles than you can shake a stick at. And they all live in the greater Seattle area, so I see them a lot."

For just a moment, Caroline allowed herself to wallow in self-pity. So much family, so close...she'd always wondered what it would have been like if she'd had a brother or sister. Then again, she wouldn't wish her childhood on anyone.

"Tell me about them," she said instead, eager to hear about life in a big family.

He sipped his coffee again, warming to the subject. "Mom's a housewife, but you'd better never put the word 'just' in front of that. She's an amazing cook, volunteers for everything, and managed to keep all of us kids in line. And believe me, that was a full-time job. My dad's retired from the force after thirty years as a beat cop. He could have gone all the way up the ladder, but had no tolerance for political games. Besides, he always said the street needed him more than a desk did."

"So you're following in his footsteps," she said, wrapping her hands around her cup. The steamy drink warmed her palms like the thought of him warmed her heart.

"Those are some pretty big shoes to fill." He shook his head. "I try, but..." His voice trailed off.

Caroline leaned forward. "I'm sure he's proud of you."

"Hope so. But we all turned out pretty well." He held up his hand and started ticking off his fingers, one by one. "Oldest brother, Dante, is a cop, too. Single dad, teenage daughter. Next is Bianca, who sells personalized gift baskets over the Internet, so she can stay home with her three kids. Paul works for Boeing; he and his wife have twin boys, both hellions. Lucky is in the Marines, Vin runs his own computer software company, and Gia—she's the baby—is starting medical school at UW."

"Wow," she said, more than a little overwhelmed by it all. "Impressive."

"You have no idea." He rolled his eyes. "It can be a pain sometimes, but for the most part I love being part of a big family."

She could only imagine the joys and trials of that many people in someone's life, joined by love as well as genetics. But she nodded anyway, because it seemed like the thing to do.

"It must be nice to be so close to your family." Swallowing, she forced a note of cheer into her voice. "So I take it you're a homeboy?"

If he heard the longing in her voice, he was kind enough to ignore it. "Born and bred," he laughed. "My parents still live in the same house in West Seattle where I grew up."

Caroline felt another twinge at the thought of belonging somewhere like that. Out of the corner of her eye, she caught Tony checking his watch. "Late for something?"

He winced. "Sorry. I have to stop by HQ before the captain takes off for the day. I hate to cut this short, though."

She waved away his apology. "Don't worry about it. I need to get back to the office anyway." At his skeptical look, she felt a sudden urge to stick her tongue out at him, but she ignored it. "I do have plenty to keep me busy, even if I don't have clients scheduled today."

"Good." He smiled at her, and she felt those butterflies flutter to life again. "I'll walk you back."

She hitched her purse strap over her shoulder. "That's not necessary."

"I know." He moved to her side, linking his arm through hers. "But I'm going to do it anyway."

଼ଠଃ

She was a woman of many contrasts, he thought as he maneuvered with her down the now-crowded sidewalk to her office. Professional and in control one minute, unable to hide the longing in her eyes as he spoke of his family the next.

She'd tried to mask it, but he had too much experience reading people to miss the sadness behind her cheerful expression. Those few sentences about her family—what little he dragged out before she tight-lipped it and turned the spotlight back on him—told him more than she probably wanted him to know.

That was okay, though. If he played his cards right, he'd have plenty of time to get her to open up.

They arrived at the door to her office, and she dug around in her purse for a minute, searching for her keys. Unlocking the door, she stepped inside, flipping the sign from CLOSED to OPEN. She crossed to her little office and tossed her purse on top of her desk. "Thanks for the break."

"My pleasure," he said, because it had been. And he hoped there would be more pleasure to come.

"So I guess I'll see you next week."

"Have dinner with me tonight," he blurted out.

She drew herself up straight. "I thought I explained myself earlier. I can't."

"I have good table manners. Come on, just dinner."

Caroline sighed. "I can either be your massage therapist, or we can go out on a date." She held her hands in front of her, as if holding an imaginary scale, and lifted one. "Professional." Lifting the other, she said, "Personal." Looking him directly in the eye, she said, "One or the other. You choose."

Hot damn. He went from semihard to hard in two-point-five seconds. Three steps took him across the room to where she stood, eyes wide, pupils dilated. Reaching out a hand, he laced his fingers through hers, and did what he'd wanted to do since the moment she walked into the dressing room at Strippendale's. He bent his head and took her mouth in a deep, searing kiss.

She gasped at his move, but didn't pull away, which he decided was a positive sign. His tongue teased the seam of her lips, slipping inside as they parted. One hand threaded through her hair, dislodging her ponytail holder. The other, still holding her hand, curved around to the small of her back, pulling her closer until they were pressed together from chest to knee.

After her initial hesitation, Caroline threw herself into the kiss as ardently as Tony had. Her tongue stroked his with enthusiasm, her hips pressing against him so tightly he groaned into her mouth.

There were too many layers of clothing between them, he decided, letting go of her hand. She immediately stroked it up his arm, wrapping around his shoulder to pull him closer. He traced her hip, hand moving lower, until it splayed over the curve of her delectable ass. He wanted to rip off her oh-so-proper business attire, lean her back over the desk and bury himself in her sweetness.

Maybe a little excessive, considering they hadn't even been out on a real date yet.

Pulling back, he dropped a kiss on the tip of her nose, taking a little satisfaction from the dazed look on her face. "No contest," he said. "I'll pick you up at eight."

Then, before she could protest, he slipped out the door, holding back the goofy grin that threatened to break free.

Chapter Four

She was being completely ridiculous.

Caroline tossed her fourth outfit of the evening on the bed, muttering under her breath. She hadn't even agreed to this date, not officially, so why was she spending so much time and effort getting ready for it?

Of course, sticking her tongue down his throat wasn't exactly a no.

Neither was giving him her address when he'd called an hour ago.

She flipped through the remaining outfits in her closet, eying them critically. Too heavy. Too boxy. Too brown. Too itchy. Too sexy.

Her hand stilled, fingering the silky fabric. She'd bought the dress months ago, loving the feel and fit of it, but hadn't found an opportunity to wear it yet. It was too feminine for work, where she usually chose well-fitting but conservative outfits that projected an air of competence and professionalism. She'd never gone for the patchouli and earth shoe look some of her colleagues enjoyed; she'd never have been able to pull it off. But she didn't want to look sexy at work, either, so her closet was sadly low on date wear.

Especially since it had been a long, long time since she'd had need of something to wear on dates.

But she'd fallen in love with the dress on first sight and spent far too much money on an item of clothing that only took up space in her closet. So why not wear it tonight?

She checked the clock on her bedside table, wincing at the time. Too late to go buy something new. Taking a deep breath, she reached into the closet and grabbed the hanger.

ஐcя

Oh, God.

She was going to be the death of him.

Her dress was a little slip of a thing, all silky-satiny and covered with blooms. It barely reached mid-thigh, long enough to be legal, short enough to be lethal. Her hair was loose again, like the night they'd met, and her eyes sparkled in a face that looked fresh and alluring, with just a touch of makeup.

He was toast.

Straightening, he pulled his hand out from behind his back. "These are for you." Then he kicked himself for stating the obvious. Why couldn't he come up with something clever?

She blushed, which did interesting things to her cheekbones and neck, not to mention the smooth expanse of skin dipping down into her cleavage. "Thank you," she murmured, and buried her nose in the blooms. He'd picked the biggest, brightest bouquet in the store, filled with a bunch of flowers he couldn't begin to identify. But they were gorgeous and they smelled great, like Caroline.

She looked at him and smiled, and just because he wanted to, he reached over and tucked a stray lock of her hair behind her ear. The flame red hair was soft and silky smooth to the touch, and he went instantly hard as it slipped between his fingers.

It was going to be a long night.

She walked into the apartment and he followed, admiring the way her skirt rose a bit as she stretched to take a vase off a high shelf. Filling it with water, she added the bouquet and primped with the flowers a little, shifting individual stems until the look was just right. Or at least Tony assumed that was what she was doing. It looked exactly the same to him. Then she placed the vase on the table behind the couch, a tiny smile curving her kissable lips.

Would she look the same after making love, sated and soft?

God, he sure hoped he'd have the chance to find out.

"I hope you like Italian," he said, both to fill the slightly awkward silence and to get his mind out of the bedroom.

She nodded. "I'll get my wrap," she said, her hips swaying gently back and forth as she walked down the hall.

Tony looked around as he waited, his hands tucked in his pockets. Her apartment was great, all hardwood floors and leaded windows, with an expansive view of the Seattle skyline shimmering in the darkness outside her sliding glass door. Bright white walls trimmed in wood sectioned off the rooms, while a river rock fireplace held the place of honor in the living room. The furniture was sleek and low key, all natural colors accented with bright patterned throws and pillows. Black-and-white photographs and abstract art dotted the walls.

Then Caroline walked back into the room, a multicolored wrap pulled over her shoulders, and all other color in the room faded to gray. Tony stood there for long seconds, staring at her, until she broke eye contact and cleared her throat, obviously uncomfortable with his scrutiny.

"Beautiful. Your place, I mean. It's stunning." So was she, but he had a feeling she would be less likely to accept that compliment right now.

"Thanks." She turned a lovely shade of blush. "It was my grandmother's. She left it to me when she died."

"Ah." He looked around with a little more interest. "Your childhood home."

"Yeah," she said. "I suppose in a way, it was."

Tony looked at her sideways, but she stopped at that. "Well, we'd better get going." He placed his hand in the small of her back. He could feel the heat of her body through the thin fabric of her dress. Closing his eyes, he asked for the strength to resist. At least until after dinner.

Yeah, it was going to be a long, long night.

ಸಿಂಡ್

Any awkwardness melted away as they chatted in the car. Tony had an easy way about him, an ability to draw her past her natural reserve and make her comfortable. They talked about everything and nothing, from the Mariners to the last play she'd seen at the Rep to the difficulties of starting a new business.

Before she knew it, Tony had pulled the car to a stop at the curb, bounding out in time to open her door and help her out. She looked uncertainly at the residential neighborhood in front of them, wondering where the restaurant might be.

Then the front door of the home opened and people spilled out, rushing forward to clap Tony on the back and herd them inside. Someone took her wrap and someone else pushed a glass of red wine into her hand, voices talking over each other in the confusion of hello. As the group started down the hall, carrying Caroline and Tony with them, she managed to grab his arm and pull him aside. "This isn't a restaurant!" she hissed, glaring at him.

"Nope."

"So where are we?"

"Mama!" Tony broke away to plant a kiss on the cheek of a plump, dark-haired woman in a tomato-sauce-stained apron. "*Come stai!*"

"*Molto bene, grazie.*" She kissed him back, then looked over his shoulder at Caroline with undisguised interest.

Mama?

With a grin, he laced his fingers through Caroline's unresisting hand and tugged her forward. "Mama, this is my friend Caroline. Caroline, this is my mother, Sofia DiMarco."

The older woman broke into rapid-fire Italian, gesturing expansively as she chattered. Tony laughed and responded in kind, shaking his head at her. Evidently she was mollified by his response, because she turned to Caroline and smiled at her. "Welcome," she said in softly accented English, kissing both of Caroline's cheeks and drawing her into the room. "I'm so glad you could join us, though I wish my son had given some advance warning."

This last was tossed over her shoulder at Tony, who appeared unaffected by her comment.

"I'm sorry," Caroline stammered. "You're not the only one who was kept in the dark. I had no idea we'd be eating here tonight."

"No apologies!" Sofia waved a hand in front of her in dismissal. "We have more than enough to eat, and one more at the table is always welcome. I only wished I could have welcomed you properly, is all."

A woman who looked to be a few years older than Tony passed in front of them, a toddler clinging to her leg. "Antonio was always bringing home guests, Mama. Why should that change just because he's a quote-unquote grown up?"

"I resemble that remark," Tony tossed back. "Besides, Mama always cooks enough for ten families. I promised Caroline a fabulous meal, and where could I find a better one in Seattle?"

Heads nodded in agreement. Moments later, Caroline was surrounded by people as his family came forward to introduce themselves. By the end of it, her head was spinning.

"I hope there won't be a test," she said, still trying to place which children went with which parents.

Tony laughed at that. "Don't worry. I'll be your personal cheat sheet."

"I'm going to hold you to that," Caroline murmured as they turned the corner into the dining room. Her eyes widened at the sheer size of the dining room table. It could easily seat twenty, which was a good thing considering the number of people in the room. As if there had been a silent signal, people started taking seats, laughing and jostling each other out of the way. Tony held out a seat for her, and she dropped into it, sure her legs would give out beneath her if she stood much longer.

He'd brought her to a family dinner.

Caroline Richards didn't do family. Even when she'd lived with her grandmother, dinner had been a quiet affair, the two of them at the kitchen table. Nothing like this loud, boisterous, amiable free-for-all at the gigantic DiMarco table.

Suddenly, Tony grabbed her hand, igniting the desire that had been haunting her all afternoon. The group gathered around the table quieted, and to her astonishment, the woman on the other side of her—Tony's younger sister, if she remembered correctly—took her other hand. Around the table hands were joined and heads bowed as Tony's father led a blessing.

Then the entire group chorused "God bless the cook!" and dropped hands, Tony giving hers an extra squeeze before letting go. The volume in the room quickly reached ear-splitting levels as people reached forward to dig into the mountain of food.

A large white casserole dish passed into her line of vision, held by the dark-haired woman to her left. "Help yourself," she said, leaving it with Caroline as she grabbed the next dish. Caroline dished up a little from each bowl and platter until her plate was overflowing with great-smelling, unidentifiable food.

She picked up her fork and took a bite, closing her eyes at the delicious taste. She may not know what it was, but she knew what she liked.

"*Saltimbocca,*" Tony whispered in her ear, his rumbly voice and warm breath sending shivers down her spine. "Veal cutlets. Roughly translated, it means 'hop in the mouth'."

Ooh. Now she was thinking about his mouth. And hopping. On him. Not a good daydream for a family dinner.

"How's your new puppy?" Tony's father took a sip of wine. "Chewed up all your shoes yet?"

"A prime candidate for obedience training." Tony grimaced. "I'm working on it, though."

"You have a dog?" She wasn't sure why, but the idea charmed her.

"Two," the brother across the table from her answered, before Tony could get a word in edgewise. "And a mangy alley cat, too."

"I do not have a cat," he protested, but the rest of the family hooted with laughter.

"You feed it, give it water, and you've made a little shelter for it on your back porch. Face it, you have a cat. You just don't let it in your house." His mother narrowed her eyes at him. "Or do you?"

Tony ignored the question and tried, somewhat unsuccessfully, to change the subject. But his brothers and sisters were more than happy to regale Caroline with stories of all the strays—animal and human—that Tony had been renowned for rescuing throughout childhood.

She took it all in, shaking her head at the thought of Tony lining a shoebox with his mother's best scarf for an orphaned robin, laughing when his brother Luciano—Lucky—described the lengths Tony had gone to in a futile effort to hide yet another puppy from his parents.

"They always knew." Tony sighed, but Caroline caught the glimpse of devilish humor in his eyes. "I could never get away with anything."

"Oh, I don't know about that," Lucky teased, one eyebrow raised, which made Caroline wonder what, exactly, Tony got away with way back when.

But the more relevant question was how much he could get away with now. She sucked in a breath as he traced delicious patterns on her thigh beneath the tablecloth.

"So, Caroline. How did you and Tony meet?" His mother was smiling, her blue eyes crinkled at the edges.

Okay, forget the wandering hands. Caroline glanced at Tony, horrified at the question. He winked at her before turning to his mom with a grin. "I arrested her." He took a bite of handmade ravioli. "Mistakenly, of course."

Caroline winced, waiting for an outcry. Instead, his mom shrugged and said, "Of course," then turned to ask Tony's little sister if she'd finished her homework yet.

137

"I'm in med school, Mama, not junior high," the dark-haired beauty teased. "Give me a little credit."

The conversation turned to Gia's course load for the quarter, with everyone weighing in with opinions on the topic. Caroline took the opportunity to gripe at Tony.

"I can't believe you said that," she hissed, eyes darting around the room.

Tony looked as well. "It's no big deal, Caroline. I just told her the truth." He gestured at his family. "As you can see, they're not shocked."

No, they weren't. If anything, the announcement had been met with a casual acceptance. She shook her head, befuddled, and more than a little charmed at the in-your-face, welcoming atmosphere of Tony's parents' house.

She glanced at Tony again, now deep in conversation with his little niece about the benefits of Barbies versus Bratz, whatever the heck they were. A body to die for, a work ethic that matched her own and a warm, generous family to boot.

If she weren't careful, she'd find herself falling for the whole package.

And that scared her more than the thought of ending up back in that holding cell.

ℬ⋑⋐

"A family dinner?"

Tony glanced over at her, a chagrined smile on his face. "It seemed like a good idea at the time. Didn't you enjoy yourself?"

She stopped short, considering the answer. "Yeah, I guess I did," she said, a little surprised to realize it was true. His family had been loud and overwhelming—and totally welcoming. It was an unusual experience, but a nice one nonetheless.

And it was pretty darned considerate of him to ask, too. Dammit.

"However," she said, eyes narrowed, "it would have been nice to have some forewarning."

"Ah, but that would have ruined the surprise." He grinned at her. Then he sobered, reaching across the seat to take her hand. "I was afraid you'd say no. And I really wanted you there tonight."

A warm glow took up residence in her middle. "Why?" she asked.

He rolled his eyes. "Because I like you? Sheesh, Caroline, that's pretty obvious, don't you think?"

Caroline was tempted to ask why again, but they'd stopped at a red light and Tony took the opportunity to lean across the front seat and kiss her.

She melted like gelato under his tender kiss, the warm glow spreading throughout her entire body. He threaded his fingers through her hair, tilting her head a little to the right as he slanted his lips over hers.

Oh, he did know how to kiss, with just the right amount of pressure, his tongue slipping effortlessly into her mouth. Her tongue danced with his, sparking flames of desire that gathered low in her belly. His other hand teased the hem of her skirt, tracing circles on the overheated skin beneath.

She leaned into his touch, legs falling open as if of their own accord, her breath coming in shallow gasps. She looped an arm around his neck, pulling him closer—

Until a sharp blast from a car horn brought her back to reality.

139

"Green light," she gasped, sitting back abruptly. She smoothed her skirt down, trying to slow the rapid beat of her heart.

Tony glanced in the rearview mirror at the lineup behind them. "Right," he growled, his jaw tight. He put the car into gear and accelerated through the intersection. Then he looked over at Caroline and smiled sheepishly. The hard planes of his face softened. "Well, that hasn't happened to me in, well, never," he said.

"I guess it could have been worse." Caroline finger combed her hair back into place.

"Yeah?"

"Could have been one of your colleagues, pulling us over for public indecency," she teased, in an attempt to rein in her libido with light conversation. So far, it wasn't working, if her accelerated heartbeat and rapid breathing were any indication.

He laughed, a breathless huff that told her he was as affected by their kiss as she was. That bit of knowledge went a long way towards calming her overactive nerves. "Yeah, that might be awkward," he agreed.

They drove a little way in silence, his hand tracing idle patterns on her bare knee. Despite the late-evening chill in the air, Caroline was about ready to break out into a sweat. The heat from his touch warmed her from the inside out, melting what little resistance she still had.

Resist? She couldn't resist this man if she tried.

And she had no intention of trying.

"What are you thinking?" His voice was low, casual, as unconcerned as the gentle fingers on her leg.

Caroline swallowed. As if she had any intention of telling him she was wondering what he'd be like in bed. "I was thinking that you're a nice man," she said instead.

"Ouch." He lifted his hand off her leg and slapped it across his chest. "You sure know how to hurt a guy, don't you?"

"What?" She laughed in spite of herself. "What's wrong with being nice?"

Tony shot her a disbelieving glance. "Nice is for little dogs and flower arrangements and restaurants you take your grandparents to. Nice is one step up from you've got a great personality. Chicks don't dig nice guys."

Caroline took a deep breath and stepped off the ledge. "I do."

ೞಐ

Oh, yeah.

Tony swallowed, recognizing that their conversation had jumped several levels from "casual date" to "serious message" in the space of one second. He'd been trying so hard to keep things easy and nonthreatening all night, instinctively knowing that Caroline was one wrong step away from bolting. It didn't take a detective to realize she'd been burned before, and ultra wary of giving too much away.

So he'd promised himself he would take it easy, let her set the pace, even if it killed him.

And it almost had, with her so soft and tempting and delectable, right next to him but off-limits. He'd spent most of the evening grateful that the tablecloth hid his reaction—from her as well as his family.

But now she seemed ready to knock down at least one of the walls of resistance on her own.

"All nice guys," he asked slowly, trying to keep his tone light, "or any in particular?"

Her lips twitched, which caused a similar reaction in his groin. "Now you're fishing for compliments."

"I'll take them where I can get them," he said. The little joke elicited a laugh from her and eased the tension a little.

He pulled his car to a stop at the curb, wishing she didn't live so close to his folks' house. He could have easily driven all night for the chance to talk to her, look at her, enjoy her unique scent, a mix of vanilla and almonds that made him crave a taste.

"Are we here already?" She sounded as disappointed as he felt, and damned if he didn't take it as a positive sign.

"Yep." He unbuckled his seatbelt. "Hang on and I'll get your door."

She reached out and put her hand on his wrist, stopping him midmove. "Wait."

Tony sat back and looked at her, hoping she was as reluctant to call it an evening as he was.

Caroline looked down at her hand, still touching his. "Would you..." she swallowed and looked up, her eyes full of trepidation and excitement and desire. "Would you like to come in for a while?"

"Hell, yeah." He cupped the back of her head with one hand and kissed her thoroughly. He pulled back, gratified to see the glaze of desire in her eyes. He knew it matched his own. "There's nothing I want more."

Chapter Five

The sound of the door clicking shut behind them was deafening in the empty apartment. Or maybe it was her nerves kicking in, Caroline mused as she dropped her keys on the entryway table. She took a deep breath and turned to Tony, her smile trembling on her lips.

"I'm not a dentist." He leaned against the wall.

"Excuse me?"

He reached out and traced the line of her jaw, leaving a trail of heat behind. "You look like you're ready for a root canal. Relax, Caroline. You're in charge. You set the pace."

"O-okay." She gestured toward the couch. "Why don't you have a seat, and I'll get you something to drink."

Tony smiled at her. "That sounds nice."

A shiver ran up her spine at the low, sexy note in his voice. She could have an orgasm listening to him read the phone book. Probably wouldn't be much fun for him, though.

"Would you like a glass of wine? Some coffee?" She could see the back of his head from the open kitchen, the way the hairs at the base of his neck curled a little, brushing the collar of his shirt.

He turned, leaning one arm across the back of the couch. "Coffee sounds great. Decaf, if you've got it."

Caroline nodded and reached for the grinder. She was so wired with sexual tension right now, a dose of caffeine would send her right over the edge.

"Anything to eat?" She wasn't sure what she could offer him, but it seemed like the polite thing to do.

Thankfully, he shook his head. "I'm always stuffed after a meal at my mom's. I'll take a rain check, though."

Caroline sucked in a breath at the implication. She covered her reaction by grinding the decaf coffee beans and putting them in the coffeemaker.

Silence filled the room, but it was a comfortable one. Tony looked around the room, his gaze falling on Caroline with thrill-inducing regularity. She fought the urge to check her hair in the shiny door of the microwave.

"So what's it like being a vice cop?" She put half-and-half and sugar on a tray, waiting for the coffee to finish brewing.

"It's great." He smiled. "Especially when you can make a difference, shutting down a prostitution ring or getting drugs off the streets."

"It must be gratifying."

Tony shrugged. "Sometimes it feels like a great big game of whack-a-mole, though. Get rid of one predator, and two more pop up to take his place. Easy to get cynical."

She laughed at that. "Cynical is about the last word I'd ever use to describe you."

"No, really." He held her gaze, his expression serious, but moments later a chuckle escaped. "Okay, you're right. I *am* an eternal optimist. But that's not to say the job doesn't get to me from time to time."

"Well, of course." She smiled and lifted the full coffee pot. "Remember, you're talking to a professional massage therapist here. I felt the stress in your shoulders."

A fine tension settled on the room as memories of her hands on his naked back surfaced. She cleared her throat, looking away.

"Yes, you did." Tony shifted on the couch. "But that stress had more to do with the knowledge that my rarely seen cynical side had encouraged me to arrest an innocent citizen."

Caroline poured two mugs of coffee. She carried the tray out to the living room, placing it on the low glass-topped table in front of the couch. "I'd assume that's not an everyday occurrence for you."

"Nope." He blew on the coffee before taking a sip. "But there's a first time for everything."

Caroline felt her pulse speed up at the thought of other firsts that might be happening tonight. "Obviously, I haven't held a grudge," she said, touching him on the shoulder. "It was an honest mistake. I just happened to be in the wrong place at the wrong time."

"Oh, I wouldn't know about that." Tony shifted toward her, the fabric of his khakis brushing against her bare knee. "Because if you hadn't been there that night, I wouldn't be here right now."

And with that, the last of her tension drained away. Stroking her hand up his shoulder to the nape of his neck, she threaded her fingers through his hair. Tugging gently, she urged his head down and covered his mouth with her own.

And as he'd promised, she set the pace. The touch of her tongue on his lips met with no resistance, and she stroked it into his mouth, teasing his tongue with little caresses.

His arm, resting on the back of the couch, circled her shoulders and drew her closer, until she was half-lying on him. She arched against him, her nipples brushing his chest, separated only by the thin fabric of their clothing.

What she wouldn't give to be naked right now, skin to overheated skin!

With that thought in mind, she wiggled around until her hands were free to start working on the buttons of his shirt. It was complicated work, of course, considering all the kissing that was going on as well, but she was willing to multitask.

He groaned into her mouth, hands stroking up and down her back in a rhythm both soothing and sensual. She nipped at the line of his jaw, darting kisses down his neck, as she worked open the buttons lower on his shirt. In response, he cupped her buttocks, pulling her into direct contact with his erection.

She could feel the heat and weight of him through his khakis, molding the silky fabric of her dress to the juncture of her thighs. Her panties were already damp, a tremor of desire shaking her.

Tony pulled back, breathing heavily. "You okay?" he rasped, his voice hoarse.

"Mm-hmm." She rotated her hips into closer contact with his, delighting in the involuntary groan that escaped him. "Never better."

"Good." Without warning, he twisted so he was sitting upright with her across his lap, grinning as she shrieked her surprise. Another smooth move and he was standing, cradling her in his arms. "Now tell me where your bedroom is before I take you right here."

༺༻

Pillows.

Tony stopped at the bedroom door and stared at the bed.

"What's wrong?" Caroline looked up from tormenting his neck with little nibbling kisses.

"Nothing." He looked around for a place to set her down before giving up and lowering her to her feet. He strode over to the bed and began pitching pillows onto the floor.

"Hey!" She grabbed one out of his hands before he could toss it. "What are you doing?"

He snagged another one and dropped it on the already-covered chair at the side of the bed. "Honey, if I don't get you on this bed naked in the next thirty seconds, I'll go out of my mind. But in order to do that, I have to find the bed first."

"Oh." Flashing him a smile, she tossed the one in her hands on the floor and joined him in the pitch-fest.

"Now," he said, twitching the comforter back, "let's work on the naked part."

In response, she turned her back to him and lifted her hair off her neck. "I need some help with my zipper," she said.

Have mercy.

With one finger, he reached out and traced the creamy skin at the edge of her neckline. He felt her tremble under his touch and bit back a groan. Taking the zipper pull, he slowly tugged it down until it ended at the curve of her waist.

A wiggle of her shoulders and it slipped right off, leaving him staring at a smooth expanse of naked skin, marred only by the scraps of lace and satin that made up her bra and panties. She glanced over her shoulder at him, a wicked glint in her eye. "Your turn."

Tony began working on his half-unbuttoned shirt, but his hands stilled as Caroline turned, placing her hands over his. "I believe that's my job," she murmured. With a deft movement, she slipped a button free.

Her hair draped over her bare shoulder, brushing against his chest as she spread his shirt open.

Stepping back, he shucked out of his pants and boxers while she removed her bra and panties.

Caroline reached out and stroked the long, hard length of him, her eyes slumberous and darkened with desire. Tony sucked in a breath, closing his eyes briefly at her delicate touch. He grasped her wrist and held it away, shaking his head with a smile. "I can't take much more," he warned her.

Caroline leaned forward to press a kiss to his bare chest. "Good," she murmured. "Because that bed is looking awfully lonely."

That was all the invitation he needed. In one smooth motion, he grasped her around the waist and lifted her onto the bed, tumbling her backward against the cool sheets. Then he crawled onto the bed beside her, wrapping an arm around her waist. Arms and legs tangled as they kissed and touched and explored.

He stroked one hand down her side, fingertips burning a trail from ribs to hip, then feathering across her upper thigh to delve into the tangle of curls nestled between her legs. Her folds were slick and heated, and she whimpered as he found her sweet spot. Shifting onto his side, he stroked her over and over until her thigh muscles clenched and her back arched, lifting her into his touch. The temptation was too great. He bent his head and tasted her.

A high, keening wail escaped her lips, and Tony slid one finger inside her as she came, inner muscles clenching rhythmically. Her head tossed from side to side, eyes closed tight. He stroked her with hand and mouth until she subsided, collapsing limp and sated on the bed. "My God," she gasped, tangling her fingers in her hair. "That was...I don't...God."

"My pleasure."

She shook her head. "Not yet," she said. "But it will be."

And with that, she rolled away from him, stretching to pull open the drawer on her nightstand. She rummaged through the drawer and pulled out a foil packet with a triumphant smile.

Tony sent a brief prayer heavenward that one of them was coherent enough to think about protection, but any rational thought fled as Caroline ripped the packet open and rolled it down the length of his cock.

He shuddered as her knuckles grazed the sensitive skin of his abdomen, muscles contracting beneath the delicate touch. She looked up at him then, her hungry gaze sending a shock of recognition straight to his gut.

She wanted him as much as he wanted her, maybe more. He didn't know how or why it had happened, but he was eternally grateful for it, anyway. He reached up and tangled his fingers in her hair, pulling her down for a deep, passionate kiss. She snaked her hand between their bodies, stroking and tantalizing with feather-light caresses, until he broke the kiss, rolled her over onto her back, and settled between her legs. Then he surged into her, one long, sure stroke that brought him almost to the edge.

He braced himself above her on shaking arms, a kaleidoscope of sensations ricocheting through his body. She whimpered in protest, wiggling beneath him, but he shook his head. "I'm too close," he ground out between clenched teeth.

In response, Caroline raised her hips, bringing him even deeper. "So am I." She stroked her hands down his back to grasp his buttocks. "Don't stop."

With a growl he barely recognized as his own, Tony pulled back and plunged into her again, entire body tensing as he carried them both to the brink.

Caroline arched up, joining him in the rhythm that grew faster and faster as they raced to completion. Suddenly, her head tilted back, eyes closed, as she began contracting wildly around him. One heartbeat, two, and he groaned out his release.

His arms finally gave out and he collapsed on top of her, reveling in the skin-to-skin contact as their labored breathing returned to normal. Long moments later, he rolled to the side, pulling her with him so they snuggled together atop the tangled sheets.

"Wow," she whispered, threading her fingers in his hair.

"Yeah," he agreed, having lost command of the English language in the last few minutes. That was okay, though, since she seemed to be in the same boat.

They stayed like that for what seemed like ages, but finally he disentangled himself and went to take care of the condom. Returning, he found her under the sheets, her naked shoulders exposed.

Caroline patted the empty space next to her. "There's room." Her expression was a charming mix of hopefulness and caution.

"Glad to hear it." He slid under the sheets and wrapped one arm around her waist. "Tired?"

"Mm-hmm." She yawned. "I think you wore me out."

He laughed softly and pulled her closer. "Believe me, the feeling's mutual." Pressing a kiss to her forehead, he closed his eyes and slid into sleep.

Caroline woke, disoriented, to darkness. The space next to her was empty, and a shadowy figure was slipping into his clothes by the window.

"Going somewhere?" Her voice was rusty with sleep, but she ruthlessly tamped down the disappointment that hovered in the background. They'd made no promises, she reminded herself. Now was not the time to be needy.

And she was more than a little disturbed at how much she wanted him to stay.

He turned at the sound of her voice, and even in the darkness she could see the white of his teeth as he smiled. "Hey," he said, crossing to her and giving her a long, slow kiss. "I didn't mean to wake you."

"I'm a light sleeper." She sat up, still holding the sheet over her chest in a belated nod to modesty.

"I wouldn't have left without saying goodbye." He smoothed her hair away from her face. "I wanted to let you sleep as long as possible before I woke you."

Caroline nodded, eyes fixed on his hands as he buttoned his shirt.

Slipping on his shoes, he leaned over to give her one more kiss. "I wish I didn't have to go," he whispered. "But if I don't let the dogs out my furniture will never recover."

She nodded again. As intimate as they'd been hours before, she felt awkward right now, naked in bed as he dressed to leave. And what was she thinking, sleeping with him on the first date? She never got that intimate that fast.

"Can I take you out for breakfast?" He was standing by the door now, obviously torn between leaving and staying. "How about I pick you up?"

Caroline shook her head, a rush of relief pouring over her. "I'll need my car for after work, but my first appointment isn't until ten. Meet you at the café across the street from my office at nine?"

"Sounds great." He crossed the room again for another kiss, his hand slipping down to cup her breast through the sheet. Her nipple beaded under his touch and she moaned into his mouth. "Damn," he growled. "If I don't go now, I'll never leave."

"I'll walk you to the door." Wrapping the sheet around her, Caroline padded down the hallway. Tony kissed her one last time before walking out the door.

Caroline turned the deadbolt, the click of the lock resounding through the silent apartment.

And the emptiness echoing in her heart scared her more than anything she'd experienced in a long, long time.

Chapter Six

"So tell me about how you ended up living with your grandmother." Tony took a bite of his omelet as he waited for her reply.

Caroline sucked in a breath, forgetting the toast she was in the process of eating. Dry crumbs lodged in her throat, setting off a fit of coughing that turned her face red.

Luckily, the café was mostly empty, so she didn't attract more than a little attention.

Tony handed her a glass of water, eyes full of concern as she took a sip and got her coughing under control. "Are you okay?"

Caroline blinked away the tears brought on by the coughing fit. "Fine," she croaked, waving a hand in front of her face.

He waited for her to get back under control, then joked, "You don't have to asphyxiate yourself to avoid the question."

"You took me by surprise, that's all." She looked down at the tablecloth.

"Why?" He reached out a hand and tilted her chin up. "Is it a forbidden subject?"

"No." She fiddled with her spoon for a minute, then looked him in the eye. "Actually, I guess in a way it has been. I don't ever talk about it."

Tony sat quietly, watching her, as she struggled her way past her innate need for privacy that had kept the truth untold for so many years.

"It's a pretty basic story," she said. If she focused on the tablecloth, she could avoid eye contact. "I grew up in Los Angeles, me and my mom in a series of crappy little apartments. Today they'd call it child neglect, or emotional abuse, or something, but it was just the way life worked, as far as I knew. Mom would try for a while, get a minimum wage job for a month or two. Then she'd get drunk or stoned and check out for days at a time, either emotionally or physically. I got really good at making mac and cheese and getting myself to school. She was more interested in her next score, or what asshole she could drag home for a week or two."

Tony nodded, his eyes full of compassion.

"But as I got older, her 'boyfriends' started paying more attention to me. Before that, I could just disappear, you know? Hide out in my room, be really quiet, anything to avoid them. They were pretty much all creepy. But when I started to develop, I knew I had to get out of there. So I scrimped enough for a bus ticket to Seattle, and showed up on my grandmother's doorstep. The rest is history."

"Jesus." He shoved a hand through his hair. "How old were you?"

"Fourteen."

"You took a bus by yourself to Seattle at fourteen?" He barked out a humorless laugh. "I see it every day, and still never get used to this crap."

"I was lucky. I had somewhere to go."

"Damn lucky." His expression was fierce, and Caroline was oddly comforted by his reaction. If he'd been around during her childhood, she had no doubts he would have protected her with his life.

"Anyway, I made it here without any major problems." She sighed. "I called my mom once I got here, so she wouldn't worry, right? Turns out she hadn't even realized I was gone."

Tony muttered something under his breath, which Caroline assumed was unflattering or profane or both, and reached out to take her hand. His thumb stroked her palm, sending currents of sexual tension thrumming through her body, combined with a gentle comfort she could barely name. "And no one ever called Child Protective Services or anything? You were on your own until you got to Washington?"

"I'm not surprised no one called CPS. I was pretty good at hiding it. No bruises, no obvious physical neglect. Even my grandmother had no idea until I showed up, since she and my mom were on the outs for most of my childhood. And when she took me in, Mom wrote both of us off completely."

"What about your dad?"

She laughed. "He took off while Mom was pregnant with me, insisting he couldn't possibly be the father. And considering her track record, it wouldn't surprise me if it was true."

"So your grandmother took you in."

Caroline looked down at their joined hands. "Yeah."

"Something tells me it wasn't much better there."

"Oh, no," she protested. "Grandmother never treated me badly. It was just a bit of an...adjustment."

"No more junkies hanging out in the living room?"

Caroline felt a smile curve her lips. "Not even close. All of a sudden I had a curfew and house rules and expectations. Of course, I also had a clean bed, a warm apartment, and a home-cooked meal every night. I got with the program pretty quickly."

"But," he prompted, squeezing her hand.

She looked away. "But she never let me forget how much she'd given up by taking me in. Never in so many words, but it was clear that she hadn't banked on raising another kid through the terrible teens. Especially since my mom was such a hellion. I think she kept waiting for the other shoe to drop, even though I tried hard to be a good kid."

"I'm sure you did," he said.

Caroline shrugged. "And to her credit, she tried, too. I think in some part of her heart she wanted another chance to get it right, after failing with my mom."

"Your mom was responsible for her own choices," he said, and she nodded.

"I know. She was trapped in her addiction, and couldn't or wouldn't get out. Grams still felt somehow responsible, though. I did, too, in a way. Both of us wanted to save her, but in the end, she had to save herself."

"Did she?"

Looking at the tabletop, she shook her head, red hair swishing in a curtain before her eyes. "She tried, but never broke free. She died while driving drunk a few years back. At least no one else was hurt."

She looked up then, eyes locking with his, and was caught breathless at the emotion in his gaze. "Not entirely true," he murmured.

"I'm fine," she protested. "I am so not playing the victim card here. I have a good life, a great apartment, close friends..." Or rather, close friend. Just Mollie.

But she'd told Tony more about her past than she'd ever told anyone, even Mollie. And she could almost feel the weight lifting from her shoulders.

"I know," he said, soothing her fingers with a brush of his thumb across her knuckles. Heat followed his touch in a trembling rush. "Being a survivor doesn't make your pain any less real, though."

Caroline swallowed and averted her eyes. The combination of empathy and desire was conspiring to send her to her knees. She pulled her hand away before weakness overtook her. "I've never told anyone about this."

"I know," he said.

"I mean, Mollie's guessed some of it, but...what did you say?"

He stood, rounding the table to where she sat. Grasping her hands, he pulled her up and wrapped his arms around her, tucking her head into the curve of his neck. "Thank you," he said simply.

"For what?" Her voice was muffled, her nose filled with the spicy scent uniquely Tony's.

"For trusting me."

And she did, even though it scared her a bit. Really, she'd only known him for a short time. How could she feel such a strong connection already?

Pulling away, she tried to put some distance between them, both physically and emotionally. "I really should be getting to work," she said, her voice a little shaky.

He nodded, pulling his wallet out and tossing a couple of bills on the table. "I'll walk you there."

"You don't have to," she protested, but he was already steering her out of the café, his arm around her shoulder.

"I know," He kissed her on the top of her head. "But I want to."

∞∞

Tony dropped his pencil on his desk and stood, antsy and distracted. Until the Strippendale's paperwork was completed, he was off the vice beat, and riding a desk was one of his least favorite parts of the job.

Necessary, yes, but boring as hell.

"How's it hanging, DiMarco?" Phillips' voice cut through the buzz of the station, halting him in his walk to the break room. "Jumped that redhead yet?"

"You kiss your momma with that mouth?" He ambled over to her desk, a smile twitching at the corners of his mouth. "This job has been a bad influence on you."

She shook her head. "Three older brothers were a bad influence on me. This job and me are a perfect fit."

He had to agree there; Kelli Phillips was an outstanding vice cop, fearless and incorruptible. Still, she was a lot of fun to tease. Unfortunately, she liked to tease back.

"I noticed you brought her business cards to the break room," she continued, a glint in her eye. "Wonder how you managed to pick those up?"

"Just helping her out a little."

"Of course you are," she teased. "Regular knight in shining armor. Plus, you've got the hots for her."

Not much he could say to that, since it was true, so he shrugged and headed for the break room again.

"I've got an appointment for tomorrow," Phillips called after him. "Want me to bring her a note from you?"

He shook his head without turning around. "I can manage my own social life, thank you."

The coffee was reaching the toxic stage, but he poured himself a cup anyway. It was a good thing he wasn't on a case right now, he thought, since lack of sleep and serious distraction were a dangerous combination.

And both could be attributed to the same source—Caroline Richards.

It still amazed him how difficult it had been to leave her bed last night. Not that he was a "gone in sixty seconds" kind of guy, but spending the night was something altogether different. Beyond intimate.

And it was a little scary how right that intimacy felt with Caroline.

Tony checked his watch, frowning at the time. Already he was counting the minutes before he could see her again.

Yeah, he definitely had it bad.

ఏ)ርঽ

"God, your hands are amazing!"

"Thanks." Caroline wiped said hands on a towel. "Glad you liked it."

Kelli sat up, taking the sheet with her and wrapping it around herself for modesty. "My back feels better than it has in years," she said, rolling her shoulders. "I could kiss you. Or Tony, for bringing your cards into the station."

Caroline put the bottle of massage oil on the shelf and smiled at Kelli. "Really, a thanks will suffice."

"Yeah, I guess kissing would be out of the question." Kelli hopped off the massage table. "And I'm guessing you'd rather I didn't kiss Tony."

"No comment," Caroline said, opening the door. "I'll meet you out in the main room when you're dressed."

Kelli's laugh followed her out of the room as she gave the cop some privacy. Turning the corner, she faltered a little when she saw her chair was already occupied.

"Hey, there." Tony lifted his feet off her desk and stood up. "I took a chance that you'd be out soon."

"Just got done," she said. She winced at the breathless little catch in her voice. How could she be so weak when it came to this man?

"Glad to hear it." He reached out and wrapped his arms around her waist. Pulling her close, he dipped his head to touch his lips to hers.

Half a second later, the gentle kiss hello had transmogrified into something a thousand percent hotter, with tongues tangling and hands stroking. Tony cupped her buttocks, lifting her pelvis into direct contact with his. The length of his erection fitted against her, grinding against her aching desire, sending shocks of need deep inside.

She lifted one leg, wrapping it around his, and threaded her fingers through his hair to hold his head in place as they kissed.

It was only a pointed cough that brought their attention to the fact that they were in the middle of Caroline's office, in the middle of the day.

And they weren't alone.

"God, get a room, you two." Kelli lounged against the doorway, arms folded across her chest. She rolled her eyes as

Caroline and Tony disentangled themselves. "It's enough to make a grown woman cry."

"That's something I'd pay to see." Tony pulled Caroline to his side. She snuggled up against him as if they were made to fit. "Enjoy your massage?"

"Orgasmic." Kelli made an exaggerated face at Caroline. "Figuratively speaking, of course."

"Of course." Caroline smiled back at her. She knew her lipstick was gone and her hair disheveled, a state she didn't let anyone see her in, but Tony's obvious pride in their—relationship was the only word for it—had left her feeling a little off-kilter.

"Gotta hand it to you, DiMarco, your usual tactics paid off this time. Glad to finally reap some benefits from your white-knight complex." Kelli dug in her bag for a rumpled check. "Here you go, Caroline. Sign me up for the same time next week, will ya?" And with a grin at both of them, she headed out the door, tossing a quick "carry on," over her shoulder as she left.

Tony shook his head, chuckling as he pressed a kiss to the top of Caroline's head. "She's a character," he said.

"Yes, she is," Caroline replied absently, eyes still fixed on the exit door.

"You may be wondering why I'm here." Tony took Caroline by the hand and led her around the desk. He sat in the chair, pulling her into his lap and nuzzling her neck. "Aside from the fact that I missed you, I wanted to see if you were free this weekend. We could go to the ocean, or maybe the San Juan Islands…"

"Sorry." Caroline shook her head. "I've got Mollie's bachelorette party on Saturday."

"Too bad." Tony gave her a little squeeze. "Maybe another time."

Caroline twisted around so she could see his face. "Tony, what did Kelli mean about your white-knight complex?"

He grimaced and rolled his eyes. "It's nothing. She likes to flip me shit."

"Tony..."

"Kelli is fond of blowing things out of proportion. A couple of dogs from the pound, a food drive for a halfway house, and suddenly I have a savior complex. Trust me, I do not always need to fix things."

"Maybe." Caroline eased off his lap and paced a few steps away. Far enough to be out of his reach. "At least consciously."

Tony crossed his arms over his chest, brows furrowed. "Excuse me?"

"Oh, come on. You don't think this was a situation that needed to be fixed?" She waved a hand at the empty office. "Innocent woman has reputation trashed by false arrest, business tanking in backlash? My client list was decimated. Now suddenly I'm the vice squad's favorite massage therapist. Not counting Kelli, I've got six of your colleagues scheduled for massages the rest of the week."

Caroline shoved one hand through her hair, thoughts whirling. She couldn't let this turn her into a victim again.

"Why are you getting so bent out of shape? All I did was put a few of your cards in the break room."

"I want to be a successful massage therapist on my own merits, not because I'm sleeping with you!" Caroline sucked in a breath, stunned at the quaver she heard in her own voice.

Tony stared at her, his mouth gaping open. "Do you really think that's what's going on here?"

"No. I don't know. I'm—" Caroline threw up her arms in frustration. "I can't think clearly when it comes to you."

"Maybe you need to stop trying to think your way through life, and pay attention to what you feel," he shot back.

Angry, confused and miserable, Caroline squeezed her eyes shut. "I think you should go now," she whispered.

Silence hovered in the room for long moments. Then she felt a soft kiss whisper across her forehead, followed by the snick of the door closing.

By the time she opened her eyes, he was gone.

Chapter Seven

"Great party, Caroline!" Dani settled down in the overstuffed chair, balancing a plate on her lap. "The food is outrageously good. Who catered?"

Caroline bit her lip. "Um, I did the food myself."

Mollie leaned over, gesturing with her champagne glass. "Caroline's an incredible cook. I told her if she hired someone else to do the food, I wouldn't attend."

"Ooh, hardball! Can't have a bachelorette party without the bachelorette," someone else tossed in from across the room.

The blonde next to the fireplace—Caroline thought her name might be Jane—groaned. "Gourmet cook and massage therapist? Good thing there aren't any guys here. None of the rest of us would stand a chance!" A round of laughter swept through the room, as the rest of the bachelorette party attendees nodded their agreement.

Caroline bit her lip and looked down, trying to compose herself. Bursting into tears at her best friend's bachelorette party was not going to happen. Pasting a smile on her face, she stood, grabbing the empty tray on the table in front of her. "Who needs another glass of champagne?"

Taking a quick head count, she wove her way through the group of women, catching Mollie's eye as she went past. The flicker of worry that passed over her best friend's face told her that her attempt at covering her emotions had failed, at least where Mollie was concerned.

Sure enough, as soon as she reached the kitchen, the swinging door opened behind her. "Are you okay?" Mollie's eyes were full of concern.

"Yeah," she said, not because it was true, but because she wanted it to be true. And it wasn't as if she had lots of privacy here in the kitchen, considering that it opened onto the living room where everyone was gathered. Now wasn't the time or place to go into her heartbreak.

Unfortunately, Mollie saw through it right away. Sometimes best friends were a real pain. "Want to talk about it?"

Giving up, Caroline shook her head. "Not tonight. But soon."

"Okay." Mollie gave her a quick hug. "I'm going to hold you to that." With a grin, she took the bottle of champagne off the counter. "I'll go keep the spirits flowing. You take a minute or two to get your spirits up."

Caroline nodded and turned her attention to the dessert tray. She'd spent the night before creating the miniature wedding cakes, decorating them with each party guest's name and a personalized design. Mollie had been a bit surprised when she asked for information on all the guests, but her list of hobbies and personal favorites had been a big help in creating the confections.

It took most of the night, but it wasn't like she was sleeping much these days anyway.

Caroline sighed. Only five days since she'd last seen Tony, but it seemed like a lifetime. He'd respected her request and left her alone, which left her both annoyed and relieved.

In the long run, she was sure this was necessary. As much as she missed him, and mourned the loss of something that had barely had a chance to begin, she had no desire to be another charity case. She'd had enough of being rescued to last a lifetime.

It hadn't felt like charity, though, when she was in his arms. And the thought of never being in them again was enough to make her eyes well up with tears.

Shaking her head at her foolishness, she crossed to the fridge and took out the chocolate-dipped strawberries.

There was enough chocolate on the menu to make even the most premenstrual partygoer happy.

Caroline was leaning over the crisper, choosing the best pears for the fruit tray, when the music started.

Startled, she reared up, banging her head on the refrigerator shelf and knocking a can of cola onto the floor. Muttering a few choice swear words, she straightened, rubbing the sore spot on the top of her head.

"Caroline, you dog!" Dani leaned over the counter that separated the kitchen from the living room, grinning delightedly. "That is one hot stripper you hired!"

"A stripper?" Caroline stared at her. "I didn't hire..." Her voice trailing off, she listened to the music pulsing through the house.

It was a theme song from a police show.

Filled with a sense of foreboding, Caroline looked past Dani into the living room. The other women were gathered in a tight group near the fireplace, leaving her no room to see. Giving up, she left the kitchen and walked slowly into the main room, where the bachelorette party guests were now hooting and hollering at the stripper posing in front of the fireplace.

"Tony," she hissed through gritted teeth. Her voice wasn't loud enough to carry over the music, but his gaze sought her out anyway. His eyes darkened at the sight of her, and despite her resolve, an answering pull tugged at her.

"Hi, Caroline." He turned down the volume on the boom box. "I understand you're having a bachelorette party tonight."

"As you can see," she replied, acutely conscious of being the center of attention.

"Great!" He winked at her, then turned to look at the rest of the gathered women. "So, who's the lucky bride-to-be?"

Mollie waved her hand, grinning like a loon. "Over here. We met at the police station, remember?"

Tony nodded. "Couldn't forget that night." The look he gave Caroline could have melted his service revolver. "And I believe that meeting came about because of a misunderstanding related to this very party."

Caroline groaned, resisting the urge to bury her face in her hands. "Tony," she warned, but he interrupted.

"You were looking for a stripper. And since I'm pretty sure you haven't found a replacement, I thought I'd live up to my side of the bargain." That said, he reached over and turned up the music, his other hand toying with the top button on his skintight shirt.

The guests shouted their approval, clapping in time with the music, but by the time he undid the fourth button Caroline had had enough.

Switching off the music, she clamped her hand around his wrist and marched him off to the hall. Mindful of the groans from her fellow party guests, she called out, "Give us a minute, okay?"

And though there was a little good-natured ribbing, everyone seemed okay with that.

With a brief, embarrassed smile, Caroline dragged Tony down the hall into her bedroom and shut the door.

"What are you doing here?" Even her anger did little to tamp down the frantic beating of her heart.

"Trying to help you out," he said, his face a study in innocence.

"By taking your clothes off in front of my friends?" And yeah, okay, that was louder than it needed to be.

"You needed a stripper," he said with a shrug. "I have some experience in that area. And I didn't want to leave you in the lurch."

"And I don't want to be rescued by you," she wailed.

Tony's eyes narrowed and he took a step toward her. "Do you still honestly think that's why I'm here?"

When she didn't answer, he sighed and turned away. "Well, in that case..." Pulling his handcuffs out, he snapped one cuff around his wrist and attached the other to the post of her bed.

"What in the world are you doing?" Caroline knew she was shrieking, but at that point she didn't care anymore.

"You think all I want is to rescue you. Like you're some puppy at the pound I need to take care of. Well, let me tell you, Caroline, you are not a charity case, and I don't think of you as a puppy."

"Of course I'm not a puppy," she snapped, hands on her hips.

"At least we agree on something." He watched her pace from one side of the room to the other. The heat of his gaze sent a warm shiver through her.

"But that doesn't explain why you cuffed yourself to my bed." She stopped in front of him and shook her head.

"So you can rescue me."

"What?"

Tony reached out and grabbed her hand with his handcuff-free one. "When people are in a relationship, they help each other. It's a balance of give and take. That's what I want with you—what I thought we were on our way to developing. I'm not here to rescue you. But I'd damn well like to be rescued by you."

"Why?" Caroline's stomach dropped, like the first moments over the top hill of a roller coaster. He looked so damn good, so vulnerable, with his shirt half open and his arm locked to her bed frame. And if her living room weren't filled with a dozen friends and acquaintances right now, the erotic images running through her mind would be well on their way to reality.

His voice turned husky as he looked into her eyes. "Caroline, I've been miserable these past few days. I know we've only known each other a little while, but I can't imagine my life without you. So I'm asking you to rescue me now." With his free hand, he dug in his pocket and pulled out a small key. "Set me free, Caroline. I'm going nuts without you."

Caroline took the key from him, a tremor running through her as her fingers grazed his. She turned the key over and over in her hand.

Stepping forward, she ran her fingers down the side of his face, delighting in the contrast of smooth skin and rough five o'clock shadow. She traced the line of his mouth, pulling back as he nipped at her fingertips. "I missed you," she whispered.

"Me too," he murmured.

She took another step closer. Tony stood there, locked to her bedframe, watching her intently. His vulnerability was enough to take her breath away. And in that moment she realized that he was truly at her mercy. She had the key. If she chose to walk away, he would be stuck.

Almost as stuck as she was, trapped in her endless loop from childhood. In trying to stand on her own, had she doomed herself to standing alone?

Not if she could help it, she thought fiercely, clenching the key in her palm. As scary as it was to be vulnerable, the thought of living without Tony in her life was even scarier.

Another step took her right up to him, so close she could feel his breath on her forehead. Threading her fingers in his hair, she tugged his head down for a kiss.

The mere touch of his lips on hers and she was lost, burning for more than just a kiss. She stroked her hands over his shoulders and back, sliding down to cup his buttocks through the tight pants of his stripping costume.

Tony looped his free arm around her waist, pulling her even closer. He rotated his hips against hers, letting her know in no uncertain terms that he was as affected as she was.

Her nipples beaded almost painfully tight, brushing against his chest through the layers of clothing that separated them. She nipped at his lower lip, then soothed it with her tongue. He growled in response, smiling against her lips before slipping his tongue into her mouth.

Aching to touch his skin, she set to work on the remaining buttons of his shirt, spreading it open and caressing his chest with wide, greedy strokes.

Tony tugged at her shirt, pulling it free of her slacks, and tried to undo the buttons one-handed. The rattle of metal reminded her that he was still attached to her bed, almost sending her into a fit of giggles. Then he cupped her breast, and the laughter fled, replaced by a deep, aching desire.

She was starting to work on the buckle of his belt when a knock at the door brought them back to reality. Mollie's voice was muffled by the closed door. "Am I interrupting?"

"Um..." Caroline turned around so she was standing in front of Tony. Considering how aroused they both were, Caroline was quite sure he'd appreciate the visual block. She started buttoning up her shirt, calling out as she finished, "What's up?"

Mollie stepped into the room, her eyes bright with curiosity. "Just wondering what's going on," she said. "But I think I've answered my own question."

Caroline winced. "Sorry about ruining your bachelorette party." A bright blush heated her face as Tony wrapped his free arm around her waist.

"Are you kidding?" Mollie grinned. "You've fueled the gossip machine for weeks to come."

"Wonderful." She looked over her shoulder at Tony, who was grinning like a cat on a canary farm. "Maybe I should go do a little damage control."

Mollie laughed. "Damage control? Your reputation has climbed five notches. Dragging the stripper off to your bedroom for a conversation—priceless!"

Caroline buried her face in her hands, mumbling, "Oh, my God," but Tony just laughed.

"Won't they be disappointed when they hear I'm not a real stripper?"

"Nah." Mollie winked at both of them. "It makes the story even more interesting."

Caroline made a move to leave the room, but Tony tightened his grip on her waist. And as her behind brushed up against his groin, she understood why.

Was she doomed to a lifetime of blushing?

"Anyway," Mollie said, "I just wanted to let you know that we're taking off."

"But it's your bachelorette party," Caroline protested. "You can't leave now."

"I can, and so can everyone else. Sorry to leave you with the dishes, but that seems to be a small price to pay."

In a tiny voice, Caroline said, "I wanted everything to be perfect."

"Oh, honey, it was." Mollie crossed the room and kissed her on the cheek. "It was a great party, and seeing the two of you together made it even better. Besides, I don't need to party all night long. I've got the man of my dreams warming my bed. Home sounds pretty good to me right about now."

"If you're sure…" Caroline's voice trailed off.

Mollie shook her head and walked to the door. "My only regret is that we didn't get to see your act, Tony."

"Sorry," Caroline said. "That's reserved for me. Right?"

Tony kissed her behind the ear. "You bet," he said. "For as long as you want it."

"That sounds promising," Mollie said. "Well, I'll let you get back to your…conversation." She paused in the doorway. "You'd better take care of one thing, though."

"What?" Caroline leaned forward.

Mollie waved at Tony's arm. "Unlock the poor man. You can lose feeling in your hands really quickly with those things. Or, uh, so I've heard." And with a wink, she left the room.

"Oops." Caroline twisted in Tony's embrace, fitting the key in the tiny lock and setting him free.

Moments later, they could hear the door to the apartment close, and Caroline knew they were alone.

"Caroline." Tony's voice was low and husky, his gaze fixed unwaveringly on her.

"Yes?"

"I meant what I said."

Caroline could feel her brow furrowing in confusion. "About what?"

"About you having me for as long as you want."

Her heart started beating double time. "I do, huh?"

"And that's a phrase I'm hoping to hear in the near future, too."

She sucked in a breath. "Maybe I'll be hearing it, too."

"Oh, yeah. We're definitely going for an equal-opportunity relationship here. And speaking of which..." With a wicked grin, he lifted her up and tossed her on the bed, stretching out beside her. With one hand, he reached out and tapped the handcuffs, setting them swinging on the bedpost. "I think turnabout is only fair play, don't you?"

Caroline took a deep breath and looked into Tony's eyes. "Sounds fair to me," she said.

With a smile, Tony trailed his hand up her arm to her wrist. He snapped the handcuff around it, pressing a kiss into her palm. "I love you," he said. Then he released the other cuff from the bedpost, threaded it through the slats of the headboard, and repeated the process with her other hand.

"I love you, too," she replied, tugging at the handcuffs experimentally. Yep, she was caught tight.

Then Tony spread her shirt open and released the catch on her bra, kissing her right over her heart, and she realized this was exactly where she wanted to be.

Tony sat up, straddling her hips, and stripped off his shirt. He hummed the television theme song, the one that had played the night they met in the club. He swiveled his hips, grinning at her as he lowered his zipper.

"My, you are a bad boy," she murmured, watching him avidly. "But you're my bad boy."

"Yes, indeed," he said. "All yours."

And that, she decided as he kissed his way down her body, was music to her ears.

Challenging Carter

Dedication

For Lucy Monroe—the best mentor, supporter, critique partner, taskmaster, and cheerleader a girl could have. I'm so lucky to call you my friend.

You said this one would be your favorite. I hope it is.

Chapter One

"You have *got* to be kidding me."

Carter looked up and smiled. "And good morning to you too, sunshine."

Dani narrowed her gaze at him, jaw set. "Don't try to sweet-talk me, you spendthrift."

Ah, so that was the issue *du jour*. Carter leaned back in his ergonomic chair, fingers laced behind his head. He kicked one foot onto the desktop. "Spendthrift. I can never remember—does that mean stingy?"

"You know damn well what it means." She slapped a computer printout on the desk next to his foot. "Reckless with money. Extravagant. Wasteful."

"Hey, now." Carter shifted his sports-sandal-clad foot slightly to the left. "Watch the prototype."

Her brow wrinkled in confusion for just a minute before she glanced down at the sandal and rolled her eyes. "New product?"

He nodded, lifting his foot off the desk. He tilted it to the right and back again. "For the spring line. This new closure we've developed is going to knock Velcro on its ass."

"If you say so." She looked dubious, which was pretty much her daily facial expression. Then she scowled again. "And don't try to distract me."

"Ah, but it's such a lovely sandal," he crooned, waving his foot back and forth, back and forth, in a soothing motion. "You're getting veeeerrry sleepy...when you wake from this trance, you will no longer be concerned with the bottom line..."

Dani pinched her lips together. Carter could tell she was trying hard not to laugh.

"So tell me, oh Mistress of the Spreadsheet." He removed his foot from the desk and rolled his chair in close enough to prop his elbows on the desktop. "What evil use of money is so offending your delicate sensibilities this fine morning?"

She leaned in and pointed at the paper in front of him. "A trip to Hawaii?"

Ah. The e-mail. Carter shrugged one shoulder. "Some of the best surfing around," he explained. "It should be a good incentive, don't you think?"

"Incentive? A weeklong, all expenses paid, luxury resort trip to Hawaii?" Her voice rose before she caught herself and lowered it again with a glance to the office door. "Do you know how much that'll cost?"

He patted her hand and stood. "Yes, I do. I checked rates online before setting it up."

"So it's a done deal." She crossed her arms over her chest. "Really, Carter, you should run these things by me first."

"Always better to ask forgiveness rather than permission." He rounded the desk to stand in front of her. Then he tilted his head down and batted his eyelashes at her. "Forgive me?"

With a groan, she dropped her head. "Why do I keep this job?"

"Because I'm so darn cute." He lifted her chin and tapped it with a mock-punch. "And I let you abuse me financially."

"It's called a budget." She drew the word out like she was talking to a five year old. "Bud-get. I'm your senior financial analyst. Paying attention to the financial bottom line is what I do. Somebody has to."

"Poor, misunderstood numbers-cruncher," he said, one hand flung dramatically over his forehead like a character in a silent movie. "A lone voice crying out in the wilderness."

"Oh, stop it." A thread of laughter laced the muttered comment.

"Trapped forever in a world with people who like to spend money..."

"Okay, Mister Spend-It-All, you might as well explain the rest of the message to me."

"What, about the Wellness Challenge?" He grinned and sat on the desk, feet swinging. "It's gonna totally shake up the culture around here."

"Yeah, that's what I'm afraid of." She straightened the jacket of her boring-as-oatmeal suit. He'd been trying to get her to adopt the casual-Friday look the rest of the staff wore at Outdoor Sports Equipment, but so far had run into a brick wall there, too. Something about making an impression on the people outside the company that she dealt with on a regular basis.

As if OSE's very healthy financial status didn't manage that for her.

He tucked his hands into the deep pockets of his khaki beachcomber pants. "I had this brainstorm," he said over her groan. "We've got a corporate membership in the fitness center downstairs—"

She held up her hand. "Don't remind me. I warned you it would be a ridiculous expense."

"Nothing ridiculous about it." He ticked off the benefits on his fingers. "Increased morale, reduced absenteeism, improved job performance. Offering membership as part of the benefits package is win-win."

"Except right now nobody's using it." She tugged her suit jacket closed.

"Yeah, well, that's what the Wellness Challenge is all about," he said. "I really want people to get the most out of the health center. I've got some ideas about new directions we can go, and they're tied to health clubs. What better way to get some input from staff, encourage healthy choices, and build a more productive team?"

"You're losing me," she warned, eyes narrowing.

"It's a point system." He rubbed his hands together. "We'll start with a work-up from a trainer, get a baseline for blood pressure, cholesterol, weight, body composition. That kind of thing. For the next ten weeks, you get points for using the health club, working out with a trainer, participating in group fitness classes. At the end of the ten week session, you get another work-up, and earn points for reductions in blood pressure and cholesterol, as well as for improving your muscle to fat ratio. The top point-earner gets the trip to Hawaii."

"What if someone chooses not to participate?"

"That's their prerogative," he said mildly. "But I don't expect many people to turn down a chance to win a trip to Hawaii."

"Having to get weighed in for a work-related activity? No, thanks."

"Oh, come on," he wheedled. "Your personal trainer is like your doctor. Your lawyer. Your priest. No one sees those numbers except the two of you. All anyone else ever knows is how many points you earned, period."

"I'm sure you'll get a good response from the staff." She picked up the e-mail printout and tucked it in her briefcase. "Count me out, though."

"Sorry."

She blinked at him. "Excuse me?"

"Your participation is non-negotiable."

"You just said employees could choose not to participate."

He shrugged. "You're different."

"Oh, you have *got* to be kidding me." She crossed her arms over her chest. "You are a lawsuit waiting to happen, aren't you?"

Carter snorted. "You're as likely to sue me as you are to join in the Polar Bear swim next New Year's."

"Hey, it could happen." She looked offended. "And the Polar Bear swim? Jump in Puget Sound on January first? You'd have to be nuts."

"It's invigorating."

"It's insanity," she tossed back. "But I already knew that about you."

"You know me better than anyone else here." He nudged her with his elbow. "Come on, Dani, you've been with me since the beginning. You've never backed down from supporting a new endeavor, even when you thought I was crazy. This Challenge is important to me. Important to where I see the company going in the next few years. I could really use your support."

She grimaced, but he knew he had her. That I-can't-say-no-dammit look was just way too familiar.

"Great!" He grabbed a brochure from his desk and slapped it into the palm of her hand before she could change her mind. "All the group fitness classes are listed on the form inside the front cover. Just sign up for one of them and turn it in. You've already got a membership, even if you haven't used it yet. Make sure you sign in before each class to get the attendance points. And you'll be meeting with Heidi on Wednesday at six."

"Heidi?"

That wrinkle between her eyebrows was too damn cute. "Your trainer."

Dani let out a low groan. "Somebody kill me now."

Carter laughed. "Hey, you never know. You might end up surprising yourself and winning that trip to Hawaii."

"Damn straight," she grumbled as she headed for the door, the flyer clutched in her hand in a death-grip. "After putting up with this nonsense for the next ten weeks, a vacation in paradise will be the least I deserve."

ಸಂಬ

Dani closed her office door, leaned back against it and pinched the bridge of her nose.

Nope, the Carter-induced migraine was still there.

Sighing, she walked over to her desk and dropped into the chair. What the hell had she done?

She snorted and flipped through the paperwork Carter had shoved into her hands. She'd done what she always did—given in.

The man could wheedle sequins off a supermodel. And, judging by his dating habits since he'd hit the big time with OSE, Inc., frequently did.

She shoved a hand through her unruly brown curls and blew out a frustrated breath. Now she was stuck doing this fitness challenge for the next ten weeks, all because of Carter.

Challenging Carter

No, that wasn't quite true. She was doing it because she was a total wuss.

One wistful look from those sexy chocolate-brown eyes, and the word "no" completely disappeared from her vocabulary.

Being in love with your boss sucked.

She hadn't always been in love with her boss. She'd been in love with her best friend first.

Unfortunately, they were one and the same.

She and Carter had been best pals through college, and when he invited her to help him start up a new business after graduation, she'd jumped at the chance to work with him. It was an opportunity to spend every workday with him, to keep their friendship going.

They were still friends, yes, but he was also her supervisor. The one time she'd been impulsive, and she ended up in a situation that made it *more* complicated for their friendship to become a romance.

Not that he'd ever thought of her that way, of course.

Dani started to crumple up the brochures for the health club. Just because he wanted her to do the Challenge didn't mean she had to do it, right?

But even as she thought it, she knew she'd end up participating. Carter could be so convincing, so enthusiastic about everything. And she had to admit, the thought of a trip to Hawaii was tempting.

More tempting if Carter would come along for the ride.

He would if she asked, she knew that much. He was always willing to help out a friend.

The sad thing was, that was all they were.

Friends.

He'd be happy to go to Hawaii with her. And then he'd take the couch, telling her that she deserved the big, comfy, king-sized bed, since she'd won.

As if knowing the man of her dreams was on the other side of the closed bedroom door, completely oblivious, wouldn't be a major loss, instead.

Smoothing out the papers, she started to fill in the blanks. Oh, well. If by some amazing quirk of fate she ended up winning the Challenge, at least she'd look better in a bikini by then. Squinting at the grid listing for the group fitness programs, she tried to decipher the acronyms for the various classes. PLTS? WTRARBC? Her finger stilled above one that looked vaguely familiar. STRPARBCS. Wait, wasn't that step aerobics?

She was probably coordinated enough for that.

Checking her Palm Pilot to make sure the time worked with her schedule, she checked off the aerobics class and signed the forms.

Then she walked out into the main office and put them in the inter-building mailbox before she lost her nerve.

༄༅

Her door was closed.

And Dani, dammit, was on the other side.

He could tell by the tapping sounds filtering through the door and the light visible under the frame. The woman never left a room without turning off the light, sometimes even when someone else was still in said room.

Okay, that only ever happened to him. She had no respect for his position and authority in the company.

Not that he'd have it any other way.

Smiling, he raised his hand to knock, when a loud beeping sounded from the other side of the door, followed by a crash and some creative swearing.

He didn't bother with the knock, just opened the door and walked in. He looked around, puzzled.

She was nowhere in sight.

"Dani?"

Another thud, this time from—under her desk? Carter crossed the room just in time to watch Dani extract herself from the tiny space between her desk and her chair.

"Should I ask?" He leaned down and held out a hand, which she took with a decided lack of grace.

"Alarm startled me," she muttered. Dropping her cell phone on the desktop, she added, "Guess I was a little too caught up in my paperwork."

Carter resisted the urge to laugh. "Caught up in her paperwork" was a daily occurrence for Dani.

"You ready to go?"

Dani looked at him, eyes narrowed. "Why do you think I'm going anywhere?"

"Your alarm was a clue."

"But you already know where I'm going, don't you?"

"Yep." He reached down and grabbed her athletic bag, looping the strap over his shoulder. "Your trainer appointment."

Dani hooked her finger through the strap of the bag and pulled it away from him. "I don't need a personal escort, thank you very much."

"Oh, come on." He wrapped an arm around her shoulders and steered her toward the door. "I'm heading that direction anyway. We can walk together."

She ducked out from under his arm when they reached the door. "Go away, Carter."

"Not a chance."

She headed toward the elevator. "And why, exactly, do you have to go down to the health club?"

"No reason." He followed her down the hall. "I needed a break."

Dani pushed the down button at the elevator button with a little more force than necessary. "You *do* think I need an escort."

"The thought did cross my mind that you'd get wrapped up in work, like usual, and miss your appointment."

"And if I did, so what? Why is this so important to you?"

Carter scrubbed a hand through his hair. "I worry about you sometimes, Dani. All work and no play..."

"If you tell me I'm dull, I'll force-feed you my gym bag."

"Of course you're not dull."

"Gee, thanks." She shook her head.

The doors opened and Carter stepped back to let Dani out, glad for the interruption. Man, she was touchy today.

"So what class did you sign up for?"

"Step aerobics." She stopped at the glass doors to the health club, squaring her shoulders. "It's right after my meeting with Heidi."

"You'll do fine." He reached past her to open the door. "I bet you'll be loving this before the end of the week."

She flashed him a weak smile. "Hope so."

Carter stopped at the front desk to show her where to sign in. Then he pointed across the room. "There's Heidi," he said. "You're good to go."

"Okay. See ya."

He grinned. "I can meet you here after your class."

"No."

"Really, it's no problem."

"Go away, Carter."

"I could even hang out *in* your class, if you'd like."

In response, she placed her hands on his shoulder blades and pushed, steering him toward the door. "Goodbye, Carter."

He was still laughing as the door closed behind him.

හඟ

The door to the exercise room stood partly open, and the sound of conversation spilled out into the hallway. Double-checking her printout from the front desk, Dani walked inside.

The space was larger than she'd expected, with a gleaming wood floor and a row of floor-to-ceiling mirrors along the far wall. Women stood around in clusters of two and three, some stretching, some just talking with friends. Dani faltered in the doorway, suddenly wishing she were anywhere but here.

"You new?" A perky blonde bounced over, a big smile on her face. "Come on, I'll help get you settled." She started leading Dani toward the front of the room, her ponytail swinging with each step. "You need to meet Jana, our instructor. She's the best."

Dani trailed in the woman's wake, glancing around as she crossed the room. Other class members looked over as she passed. Jana was fiddling with the stereo system as they approached.

"I'm Brenda, by the way." The blonde tugged Dani forward by her elbow. "Hey, Jana, you've got a new victim."

"Go away before you send her screaming from the room," Jana deadpanned. Turning to Dani, she said, "It's really not always a madhouse in here."

"Yes it is," stage-whispered Brenda, before scampering away with a laugh.

Dani handed Jana her paperwork. "I'm, uh, doing this for the OSE challenge."

"Good for you! Love to see people trying new things." Jana scanned the computer printout. "Looks pretty standard. Just bring your form with you each time and I'll sign off at the end of class."

"Thanks." Dani looked around. "Do I need anything else or…"

Jana shook her head. "Nope, just make sure you wear something comfortable and easy to remove. This class is all about your comfort level, so only go as far as you want to. No pressure. And if you have any questions, just let me know." She glanced up at the wall clock. "Oops, gotta start. Why don't you find an open space and follow along. Don't worry if you don't get every move down right away. You'll get there." With a smile, she turned away.

As Jana clapped her hands for attention, Dani looked around the room. Brenda was in the left hand corner, waving.

I've got a spot, she mouthed, gesturing at the open space next to her.

Brenda was stretching her arms above her head as Dani approached. "We always start with some warm-ups," she said. "You might not think of injuries in a class like this, but they do happen if you aren't careful."

"Mm-hmm." Dani winced as she tried to touch her toes, her fingertips barely brushing the tops of her athletic shoes.

Jana had finally gotten the stereo system working, and a sensual, beat-driven song filled the room. Standing in front of the mirrored wall, she began rolling her head from side to side. "Stretch those muscles," she called over the music. "You want to be enticing, not injured."

Enticing?

Dani tilted her head down, then rolled it to the left, grimacing as her neck popped with the motion.

"Ooh, sounds tight," Brenda said. She stretched an arm over her head, bending at the waist. "Don't worry, you'll limber up in no time."

Dani nodded as she twisted and bent and stretched, trying to keep up. If she was this far behind during warm-ups, how was she ever going to manage the step routine?

"Everyone to the floor," Jana called, and Dani joined the rest of the class in scrambling to find a spot on the polished wood boards. As she reached toward her toes, feeling the stretch throughout her body, she glanced around.

Where *were* the steps, anyway? It's not like they'd need them during the warm-up, but except for a box of free weights in the back of the class, the space was empty of equipment.

Something didn't add up.

It was a popular class, if the full room was any indication. The group was all female, from tight-bodied twentysomethings to one woman who looked old enough to be Dani's grandmother.

"Okay, now, I want you to roll slowly back up, one vertebra at a time, until you are in a seated, upright position." Jana, stretching forward between her widespread legs, demonstrated the slow position change. "And as you move, slide one hand up your leg, over your hip, across your torso, ending with it in your hair. Come on, be sexy, ladies!"

Dani blinked in surprise. Sexy? In an aerobics class? She glanced furtively around, startled to see her classmates following the instructions with enthusiasm.

"Now lean back on your elbows and bring your legs together. That's it, perfect!" Jana stood and began to circulate around the room, helping the women get into position. "You guys are totally ready for a floor routine."

She struck a pose, pulling her shoulders back. "Here, thrust your breasts out. You're hot, you're ready, you're giving him the biggest boner of his life!"

Oh, my God. Dani, who had just managed to struggle into position, sat upright. She did *not* just hear that.

Did she?

A movement to her right caught her eye and she turned, jumping a little when she saw her instructor right next to her.

Jana crouched down, a patient smile on her lips. "Everything okay? I know it can be a bit overwhelming the first day."

"I, uh..." Dani wished she didn't blush quite so easily. "I guess it's not quite what I expected."

Jana nodded sympathetically. "Getting used to being sensual in front of other people can be a bit of a challenge."

Sensual? *What?* "Well, I mean, I just thought it'd be more aerobic."

"This is only the warm-up. It'll be plenty aerobic once we get into the main routine."

Dani bit her lip. "Is that when we get the steps out?"

"The steps?" Jana's forehead wrinkled in confusion. "We don't use any steps."

"Then why call it step aerobics?"

Jana tossed back her head and laughed. "Oh, honey, you poor thing! You thought you signed up for step aerobics?"

Dani nodded, her blush rapidly turning crimson.

"This isn't step aerobics. It's strip aerobics." Jana patted Dani on the shoulder. "But I hope you'll decide to stick around anyway."

Chapter Two

"So, how was it?"

Dani looked up from her lunch. "You suck."

Carter laughed and took the seat next to her. The breakroom was almost empty at this hour, only Dani and a couple other employees still eating. "Two-thirty. Early lunch for you today."

She spooned up another bite of yogurt. "I don't want to exercise on a full stomach. Have I mentioned that you suck?"

"I believe it's come up a time or two." He picked through her lunch. "Non-fat yogurt, tuna and crackers, and a bottle of water. You're taking this challenge seriously."

"I take everything seriously."

And wasn't that the truth. "It's supposed to be fun, Dani."

"Maybe for you." She looked around the breakroom. "Or the other company employees. People who actually like working out. For me, this is sheer torture."

"Really?" He leaned back in his chair. "All those endorphins do nothing for you?"

Dani shot him a disbelieving look. "I didn't even get to the endorphins. Too busy trying not to look like a complete idiot."

"I'm sure you didn't look like an idiot."

"Yeah, right."

"Hey, it was your first day. It takes a while to get in the swing of things."

"Do I *have* to take a group fitness class? Can't I just work out on my own?"

Carter shook his head. "Sorry, babe. You have to do both, not one or the other." He eyed her more closely. "But you could change to another class if this one isn't working for you."

To his surprise, Dani looked a little annoyed at the suggestion. "Why would you say that?"

"I don't know." He shrugged. "You were complaining, so..."

"Maybe I want to take this class." She narrowed her eyes at him. "Or are you trying reverse psychology on me?"

What?

"Do you think I'm not good enough for str—step aerobics?"

"Whoa, whoa, whoa." He held up his hands. "Turning a little intense on me, here."

"Sorry." She took a bite of cracker, grimaced and tossed the rest of her lunch in the garbage. "I can't eat chocolate, I get a little testy."

Carter leaned back, balancing on the rear two legs of his chair. "So you *don't* want to take this class, but you *do* want to take this class. Makes perfect sense to me."

"I never claimed to make sense." She wrinkled her nose. "I just don't want to make a fool out of myself."

"I've got it." Carter stood, digging in his pants pocket as the chair clattered to the ground. "The perfect solution."

"And that would be..."

"Practice." He held up a key triumphantly. "You'll be head of the class in no time."

"Carter, what are you talking about?" She sounded weary. The Wellness Challenge must be taking more out of her than she'd expected.

"I'll get you into the club after hours, and you can practice the routine on your own until you're comfortable with it."

"Should I even ask how you ended up with a key to the health club?"

He winked at her. "I wrote it into the contract."

"Why?"

"So I can work out when I feel like it, especially after a long night in the office."

"Oh." She eyed the key, suspicion coloring her gaze. "So you can get me in there, no questions asked."

"Sure."

"And I'd just have to make sure the door locked behind me when I left?"

He drew back, frowning. "You wouldn't be there alone, Dani."

"But you just said…"

"I'll hang out until you're done."

She was already shaking her head. "No. No way, Carter. Not gonna happen."

Carter blew out a frustrated breath. "Not in the aerobics room, Dani. The whole point of this is for you to get comfortable with the routine without an audience."

"So what would you do while I was practicing?" She started gathering up the remnants of her lunch. "Sit in the lobby?"

"Probably a weights workout." He struck an exaggerated pose. "Have to keep my young and girlish figure, you know."

Dani burst out laughing. "You're insane."

"Yeah, I've heard that." He dangled the key in front of her. "Come on, whaddaya say?"

She raised one eyebrow. "I'll be on my own during the workout?"

He swiped a finger over his chest. "Cross my heart and hope to die."

She was wavering, he could tell. Her gaze kept straying to the key in his hand.

Carter stood. "I'll meet you at the club at quarter to nine. You can get the workout tape from your instructor before they close up, and I'll clear everything with the front desk. Once everyone leaves at nine, you can practice to your heart's content."

Then, before she could object, he left the room.

She'd be there. If only to have the last word.

ಸಿ‍ಲ್

Dani pulled the door of the aerobics room shut behind her. Just as promised, Jana had set up a TV with a strip aerobics DVD in the corner for Dani to use for practice.

"A little extra practice is a great idea," she'd said when Dani called that afternoon. "You'll be stripping with the best of them in no time."

Dani rolled her eyes and walked over to the TV. Yeah, right. She was about as far from stripper material as it was possible to get. She was reduced to giving herself homework, for heaven's sake.

Even now, she wasn't sure what had made her decide to stick with the class. Though she'd been ready to drop strip aerobics like a hot brick earlier in the day, something had changed with Carter's flip dismissal. He didn't even *know* she was taking strip aerobics, but she'd been suddenly furious that he thought she didn't have what it took. That she wasn't coordinated enough, talented enough, hell, even sexy enough.

Stupid, predictable, reverse-psychology response, but there it was. She was going to prove she could do it, damn the odds.

The most annoying thing about it was, Carter would never know if she succeeded or not. It wasn't as if she'd ever give him a demonstration.

She laughed, startling herself with the sound. She glanced at the door, aware that the club had a curiously empty feel to it, now that everyone had gone.

The clang of a weight bar dropping into place reverberated through the empty club. Correction—almost everyone had gone.

Somewhere out there, beyond the aerobics room, Carter was lifting weights.

Dani squeezed her eyes shut, trying to block out the image from earlier this evening. She'd shown up right at quarter to nine, swearing at herself for giving in to Carter's taunting but unable to back down from the challenge.

He'd already been there, flirting with the girl at the front desk, when she walked in the door. To his credit, he'd cut the conversation short immediately and walked over to her, a big smile on his face.

She was such a sucker for that smile.

At least, that was what she told herself as she followed him into the club. It sounded more appropriate than admitting that she was a sucker for his ass, too.

Really, it should be illegal for him to wear shorts like that. Her gaze kept straying below the waistband as she walked a few paces behind him. They cupped his tight ass as closely as she wanted to. Plus, they left miles of long, lean, muscled legs bare for her to appreciate, too.

And don't even get her started on his arms...

Luckily—or unluckily, depending on your point of view—he reached the workout room before she really embarrassed herself.

"How long do you think you'll need?"

Years.

"Oh, maybe an hour," she said, glancing at her watch.

He reached over and slid it from her wrist, leaving a trail of goose bumps in his wake. "Take all the time you need."

She frowned at her empty wrist. "I think that's what *you* just did."

Carter stuffed the watch in his duffel bag. "I'll just put it in my locker for safekeeping."

"Thanks. So what are you going to do while I'm practicing?"

"Free weights," he said. "Maybe some crunches. Don't worry about me. I'll have plenty to keep me occupied."

She nodded, glancing around at the almost-empty club. The sheer volume of exercise equipment was overwhelming. "I'll find you afterward."

He'd walked off with a nod and a smile, striding forward like a man who had the world at his feet.

While she had a strip aerobics workout video and absolutely no coordination.

Sometimes the world just wasn't fair.

Sighing, Dani turned on the TV. The room seemed bigger with no one else in it, and the reflection of herself in the mirror was distracting, to say the least. She eyed herself critically as she waited for the DVD to cue up to the main menu.

She wore a loose T-shirt over a white T-back sports bra, with gray yoga pants to round out the look. Fairly typical for working out, and hardly sexy. That wasn't her goal, of course; the strip video was just for exercise, not turning anybody on.

It wouldn't have bothered her to look a little more enticing, though. After all, it wasn't like it had escaped her attention that Carter had reserved his flirting for the hottie at the front desk.

Wrinkling her nose, she pulled the scrunchy out of her ponytail and let the thick brown curls swing free. Better.

She glanced back at the TV. The DVD was cued up, so she punched the start button. As the slow, sensual music started to play, Dani rolled her shoulders back and forth, trying out some of the warm-up exercises she'd learned the day before.

This part wasn't so bad. She bent over at the waist and dangled her fingers above the floor, rolling her eyes as the model in the video planted her palms firmly on the ground. Limber, Dani wasn't.

Still, it was a real workout, despite the shock-value theme. Muscles she couldn't even name protested as she bent and stretched, reached and twisted. It was obvious she'd gotten her money's worth from the workout the day before. And the music was catchy. If she could just stay on the warm-up portion of the video, she'd be fine.

For a moment, she was tempted. Why did she need to learn the strip routine, anyway? Really, there was no reason for her to stay in the class. The club offered dozens of options, all of them less embarrassing than strip aerobics. Why in the world was she forcing herself to stick it out?

Her first instinct, when Jana had corrected her mistaken impression of the class, had been to book on out of there as fast as possible. A strip aerobics class? Were they crazy?

But another look around had verified that no one in the class looked the least bit insane. They were young and old, model-thin and, well, not. And all of them were at varying levels of skill. It was like any other exercise class Dani had ever seen.

But beyond that, these women were comfortable with their bodies. They stood up straight and proud, grinning into the floor-length mirror as they went through the routine. There wasn't even much actual stripping involved; some of the T-shirts disappeared, leaving their owners in just a sports bra, but that wasn't any more revealing than a bikini.

It was the attitude that was so captivating to Dani. Strong, positive, reveling in their sensuality.

She'd wanted to leave, but in the end she'd stayed. And though the routine was way beyond her limited exercise skills, the enthusiasm of the group spilled over onto her until she'd found herself promising Jana at the end of class that she'd be back next time.

By morning, she'd changed her mind again, ready to drop out. Then she'd talked to Carter and decided to stay in the class.

So here she was, practicing in advance for tomorrow.

The warm-up music segued into a faster tune, matching Dani's heartbeat. The woman on the video smiled and paced out the first few measures of the routine, taking it slowly enough for Dani to keep up.

She followed along as the routine got more complicated, taking the time to go back once or twice to get a better look at the movements. The blatantly sexual moves were embarrassing at first, but as she kept at it, Dani found herself enjoying it more and more.

Slowly she rotated her hips, watching the movement in the mirror. It looked almost—sexy, she thought, trying it again.

She lifted her hair off her nape, letting the cool breeze of the fan tickle her. The shiver that ran down her spine was positively orgasmic.

A knock at the door sent her heart rate into orbit. She spun around, wrapping her arms around herself.

"You about done in there?" Carter's voice was muffled. "It's getting close to ten."

She darted over to the TV and shut it down, heart pounding. If he'd walked in...

"I'll be out in a minute," she shouted, taking out the DVD and putting it in its case. "Hang on."

She scurried over to the door and opened it, her heart doing a slow flip at the sight of Carter lounging against the wall opposite. Sweat dampened the neck of his T-shirt and glistened at his temples. He held out a bottle of water to her. "Just in case," he said.

She uncapped it and took a long swallow, enjoying the cool liquid. "Thanks."

"No prob." He handed over her watch and waited for her to put it on. "Hope I didn't cut your workout short."

"No. I was ready." Fighting a blush, she started for the door, not waiting to see if he'd follow. As she expected, he caught her in just a few strides, and they walked side by side out of the gym.

"So, I was thinking..."

Dani looked at him sideways. "That sounds ominous."

He stuck his tongue out at her. "Why don't we make this a standing date?"

Her traitorous heart fluttered at the word *date*. "What do you mean?"

"If you want to keep practicing after hours, I'd be happy to join you." At her frown, he clarified, "At the gym, not in your aerobics room. We'd each be doing our own thing."

"I don't want to impose," she said, though the thought of running through the routines at her own pace was tempting.

He elbowed her gently. "Dork. If it was an imposition, I wouldn't have offered."

Impulsively, she said, "Okay, let's do it."

Then she headed for the parking garage with him, wondering just what she'd gotten herself into.

Chapter Three

"I think that's everything." Carter glanced around the boardroom at the executive team. "Anything to add?"

Joe nodded. "Can we put the winter line on next week's agenda? The design team's come up with some new snow gear with built in locators, and I think the advertising team should have extra time to prep for the campaign. It'll sell like crazy, as long as people know about it."

"Good idea." Carter jotted it down on his notepad. He looked over at the head of advertising. "Thom, can you bring some preliminary workups by then?"

"You bet." Thom leaned back in his chair. "We need to look at the spring catalog, too, if there are any new developments."

"Got it." Carter wrote that down, too. "Okay, that should do it. Hope to see everyone at the annex tonight."

The noise level in the boardroom increased as the executive team stood to go, chairs scraping on the tiled floor. The hum of conversation rose and fell as people left the room in twos and threes, until Carter was alone in the room.

A quiet cough pulled his attention to the doorway. Dani stood there, manila folder in hand.

"What's up?" Carter sat down again, waving a hand at the seat next to him. "You look like a woman with something on her mind."

She tapped the folder on the table. "It's about this expense request."

With a grimace, he plucked the folder out of her hand. "I'm not going to like this, am I?"

"Explain to me how a trip for two to Vegas is a legitimate expense," she said. "I've already given in on the Hawaii thing, so don't try to tell me it's another incentive."

"Nope." He leaned back and laced his fingers behind his head. "Trade show next month. We're going to be meeting with the big box reps, as well as some potential investors."

"We as in..."

"You and me."

Dani stared at him. "You're taking me to Vegas?"

"You bet." He grinned. "Get it? Bet?"

She groaned at the bad pun. "Carter, don't make me hurt you."

"Seriously, I need you there. These guys are the big guns, Dani. They'll want specific information on our financial status, and a printout just won't cut it. I need you to answer their questions, walk them through the budget and financial forecast."

He could almost see the calculator clicking away in her head. "And both of us need to be there?"

"I don't see another option."

Dani took the folder back and flipped through it. "Okay. Any way we could cut costs?"

"What's so expensive? Two plane tickets, two registrations, two hotel rooms." He turned around and waggled his eyebrows at her. "Hey, we could make it one room, save a few bucks that way."

Instead of laughing, like he'd expected, she looked away. "Right," she said with a wry twist to her voice.

Strangely unsettled, Carter looked at Dani. "Hey, just kidding. You're like family, Dani. I'd never mess that up."

"Uh-huh." She turned to go. "I know."

"So if you're worried I'll try to take advantage of the situation or something…"

"Nope." She flashed him a tight smile. "I know you'd never do anything like that."

"Good." Satisfied, he stood and walked over to the window. The city street below was already starting to get crowded as the workday wound to a close. "Getting late. Are we on for tonight?"

"Tonight?"

He turned around. "At the health club."

She shook her head. "You've got Payday Party at the annex, remember?"

Oh, yeah. "Well, tomorrow then."

She gave him a quick wave and disappeared around the corner. Carter shuffled some papers, clearing off the conference room table. How had he forgotten? He loved grabbing a beer with most of the admin staff down at the corner bar. They did it every month on payday. It was a great team-building activity.

So why was he wishing he could skip the whole thing for a chance to work out down the hall from Dani?

ಊಆ

"Knock, knock." Caroline walked into Dani's office, carrying a padded contraption. She placed it on the floor and dropped into the chair across from Dani's desk, sighing dramatically. "I think my hands are about to fall off."

Dani laughed and shut the door to her office. "Lots of sign-ups today?"

"I swear, the number of people on that list doubles every week." She held up a hand. "Not that I'm complaining. This is the best gig in town."

"I'm glad to hear it." Dani sat back down and tapped a pencil on her desktop. "It's one expense I was happy to approve."

"My business appreciates it." Caroline grinned. "Carter's been great at talking up the in-office program, too. I've had three more companies sign up this month."

"Great." Dani forced a smile at the mention of Carter's name. Then she changed the subject. "How's Tony?"

"Fabulous." Caroline's face lit up, just like it always did at the mention of her new husband. "Do you want to come over for dinner next week? We'd love to have you."

Dani smiled wryly. "Make it six weeks from now, and you've got a deal."

"Six weeks? Even you can't be that busy."

"No, but until I weigh out for the Wellness Challenge, I have to stay far, far away from your husband's tempting cooking."

"Wellness Challenge?"

Dani waved a hand. "Work out and eat right for ten weeks, and the person with the best stats by the end of the Challenge wins a trip to Hawaii."

Caroline sat up and looked closer at Dani, one eyebrow raised. "I hope you've picked out a bikini, because you are so going to win."

"It's only been four weeks, but…" Dani's voice trailed off as Caroline urged her out of her chair and made her turn around.

"Oh, yeah." Caroline nodded her approval. "What have you been doing? You look fabulous!"

Dani blushed. "Oh, this and that." At Caroline's pointed look, she mumbled, "Strip aerobics."

"You're kidding me!" Caroline grinned. "Introverted Dani? Strip aerobics? I love it!"

Dani bit her lip, trying not to smile. "So do I."

"That's pretty clear. Not only are you looking more fit, there's this whole, I don't know, confidence about you." Caroline winked at her. "Has he noticed yet?"

"Has who noticed?" Dani prayed her blush wasn't noticeable.

"Don't try to con me, Dani Williams." Caroline crossed her arms over her chest. "You've been in love with Carter since I met you. Probably before that, too."

"Fine." Dani frowned. "No, he hasn't noticed."

"Is the man blind?"

"I don't think he'd notice if I showed up at work naked."

Caroline burst out laughing. "Honey, that's just not possible."

"Do you know what he told me today?"

Caroline sat, elbows on her knees. "This oughtta be good."

"He said he's taking me to Vegas!"

"That creep!" Caroline bit back a grin. "How could he?"

Dani shrugged. "Okay, it's not heinous. But it's not great, either."

"Going away to the city of sin with your dream guy? What's not to love?"

Dani ticked the reasons off on her fingers. "It's for work, not play. He only needs me there to talk money with some big mucky-mucks. But the worst was telling me we could share a room to cut expenses because I'm just like a sister to him."

The smile vanished. "Yep. Heinous." Caroline pulled out her cell phone. "I think it's time to call in the big guns."

Dani waited as Caroline dialed.

"Mollie?" She paused. "Can you meet us at the downtown Nordstrom's in half an hour? Great." She flipped the phone closed.

"We, who?" Dani glanced at her watch. "It's the middle of the afternoon!"

"And you need some serious retail therapy," Caroline retorted.

Dani started to argue, but closed her mouth instead. Why not? She put in more than enough hours to take off a little early today. "Okay, let's go."

Caroline grinned. "I knew I could talk you into it." She hefted her tabletop massage unit with one hand and slung her other arm around Dani's shoulders. "When we get done with you, Carter won't know what hit him."

ℰℴℛ

Carter placed the hand weights back in the rack, pausing to run a towel over the back of his neck. Ten more minutes on weights, and he'd hit the treadmill.

Other than the one night he'd missed because of the Payday Party, he and Dani were still keeping to their after-hours workout sessions. Already they were on the downward slope of the Wellness Challenge, with only three and a half more weeks to go.

Back in the aerobics room, Dani was running through her routine, which she guarded as closely as the crown jewels. He shook his head, laughing a little. She insisted the extra workout sessions were helping immensely, but he had to take her word for it. The door to the workout room was always firmly closed.

Well, whatever floated her boat. As long as she was happy, he was happy.

The workout challenge seemed to be working its magic on Dani as well. Her attitude had changed a hundred-eighty degrees. She actually seemed positive about the whole thing, and tonight she'd even mentioned how much she looked forward to their nighttime workouts.

Truth be told, so did he. Some might think it was odd to exercise that late at night, but it worked for them. They'd even taken to carpooling on workout days, giving them a little more time to just chat on the way home.

They'd always been good friends, though with work as crazy as it had been the past few years, they hadn't spent a whole lot of time together. The friendship had just been there, in the background, like the sun rising in the east. Their recent time together had brought it back to the forefront.

They'd been friends for so long, he couldn't even imagine what his life would be like without her in it. Thank God he'd never have to find out, either. Though his relationships with women tended to burn out quickly, Dani had been one of the most stable and long-lasting influences in his life. Probably because they'd never hit the sheets. He'd never wanted to risk their friendship for something temporary.

Dani's new fitness routine had given her a boost of confidence that spilled over into work, as well. She'd never pulled punches with him, of course; they had too much history for that. But she'd found it easy to sequester herself in her office, buried in her paperwork. This past month, though, he'd seen her in the breakroom at the normal lunch hour more than once, interacting with other employees. She'd even gone out after work one night last week with some of the women in research and design.

It was nice to see her finally coming into her own.

Though she'd probably kick his ass if she knew he was even thinking these vaguely paternal, patronizing thoughts about her.

Smiling again, he headed for the treadmill. He was so lucky to have Dani around to keep him honest. And with a little luck, she'd be around for a long, long time.

֍

Dani pushed her hair out of her face, tendrils curling at the temples. Say what you wanted about strip aerobics, but it was definitely a real workout.

She'd never thought of herself as an enthusiastic athlete, but something about strip aerobics had caught her. She'd gone from an embarrassed wallflower to one of the stronger students in class in just over a month.

Of course, the three-times-a-week individual workouts helped.

She'd worked her way through the first two videos in the series and was spending this week on the third, the fantasy and role-playing one. She'd even brought a button-down shirt with her tonight, replacing her usual T-shirt for a change of pace.

Slim, stretchy shorts completed the look, for ease of movement. And, if she was being totally honest, they just looked sexier.

She toyed with the top button on her shirt, swiveling her hips. She felt sexier, more in touch with her body, than she ever had before.

Onscreen, the instructor was walking her "class" through the routine, a sexy librarian role-play. "Change it up," she encouraged, bumping and grinding. "Make it *your* fantasy, *your* desires. What turns you on? Who turns you on?"

Unbidden, an image of Carter popped into Dani's mind. He was stretched out on a bed, one leg bent at the knee, as he watched her dance.

She'd imagined the two of them together before, fantasized it in the dark of the night when she couldn't sleep. But in all those scenarios, he'd been the one to take control.

In this fantasy, she called all the shots.

A flash of heat arrowed through her at the thought. To have him at her mercy, his body aching for hers, while she teased and taunted and aroused him—she clenched her thighs together at the unexpected rush of warmth.

In real life, she might never dare to show him how she really felt. But here, in this room, she could do anything she wanted.

The woman on the video slid a hand down her side, emphasizing her curves. "Don't be afraid to touch yourself," she said. "He's watching you. Show him what you want."

Slowly, Dani closed her eyes. Threading her hands through her hair, she lifted the weight of it off the nape of her neck. She breathed in slowly, reveling in the unfamiliar sensation of cool air on her sweat-dampened neck. One hand trailed down her neck, stroking across the curve of her breast as her hips swayed. Her breath grew shallow and her nipples tightened as she imagined the heat in Carter's eyes as she palmed the hollow of her stomach.

She echoed the motion with her other hand, letting her head drop back and her hair swing from side to side. As she bent at the knees, she stroked her hands between her thighs, barely skirting the aching flesh above. Using her hands, she mimicked a movement the instructor had used in the routine, pressing her legs apart and back together in one smooth movement. Slowly rotating to face the other direction, she repeated the motion. Then she straightened her legs so that her ass was lifted high, like a pin-up from the fifties.

Mmm. She was starting to like this.

Dani flipped her head back, curls tossing over her shoulder, and trailed her fingertips across overheated skin as she moved back into a standing position.

Her hands reached for the top button on her shirt. Tugging it free, she ran a finger down the open vee. Swiveling her hips, she popped one button after another until it hung open, leaving her bare except for her sports bra. She gathered the fabric in her hands and stripped it off, tossing it behind her.

But she didn't hear it drop to the ground. Opening her eyes, she glanced in the mirror.

Carter was standing in the doorway to the room, mouth gaped open, her discarded shirt clutched in his hand.

Chapter Four

Holy shit.

"Dani?"

It was her. Of course it was her. He'd left her in this room not an hour earlier, and everyone else had gone home. It had to be Dani.

He just wasn't sure when the aliens had abducted her and replaced her with this—this living, breathing embodiment of sex.

He'd poked his head in the door, meaning to check on how she was doing. But instead of finding her squinting at a TV monitor, half a step behind as she unraveled the secrets of aerobics, he'd walked in on her taking her clothes off to the beat of the music.

She stood there now, eyes wide with horror. "What are you doing here?"

He simply stared. It was all he was capable of doing. Where did she get that figure? And how in the hell had he never noticed it before?

Dani's cheeks flushed and she crossed her arms over her chest, trying to hide the fact that she was wearing just a sports bra and he was holding her shirt. "How long have you been standing there?"

A heartbeat. A lifetime. Dropping her shirt on the ground, he muttered, "Long enough."

Then he strode across the room and kissed her.

It was a crazy, impulsive act, but the minute his lips touched hers he knew it was the right thing to do.

She tasted like sex and sin and forbidden fruit, and he couldn't get enough.

Which was crazy, because this was Dani, his buddy, his pal, someone he'd never even considered kissing before. But from the moment he'd seen her tight little ass thrust up toward him like an offering from the gods, he couldn't wait to get his hands on her.

Threading the fingers of one hand through her hair, he tilted her head a little. Without conscious thought, he stroked his tongue into her mouth, and after a moment's shocked stillness Dani met the invasion with enthusiasm.

Oh, thank God.

Smoothing his hand down her back, he cupped her backside in his palm and urged one leg up and around his waist. Pulling her closer, he angled his hips so his aching cock was pressed right between her thighs. He groaned at the contact. Only a few thin layers of fabric separated them, and by the breathy little gasps she was making, he guessed that Dani hated those layers as much as he did.

Carter wasn't sure what he'd been expecting, but it sure as hell hadn't been this enthusiastic response. Her hands were everywhere, on his shoulders, stroking his biceps, clutching the fabric of his shirt. Her body rubbed up against his as she kissed him back, her lips voracious, her tongue hot and wicked in his mouth.

Sliding his hands up her sides, he caught the edges of her bra with his thumbs and tugged, breaking off the kiss long enough to strip it off of her and toss it away. Her eyes slid closed and her head tilted back as he cupped her breasts, his thumbs strumming the nipples to tight little buds.

It was too tempting. He leaned down and sucked one into his mouth.

"Carter," she breathed, one hand tangled in his hair, holding him closer as he laved the sensitive flesh. He drew a path across her chest with his tongue, tracing around her other nipple before clamping his lips over it as well.

Her hands tugged blindly at his shirt, trying to pull it up and off him. He stepped back just long enough to oblige her, wanting the sensation of skin on skin as desperately as she did. They both sucked in a breath as his hair-roughened chest brushed against her sensitive breasts.

"Damn," he whispered. Her hips arched against him in time with the music, bringing him to the ragged edge of his control.

It wasn't enough. He needed more.

The elastic waist of her shorts was easily breached, and he slid his hand inside. "God, you're wet," he groaned, stroking one finger through her damp folds. She was tight, so tight, and he clenched his jaw against the hot pleasure of her inner muscles' gripping him.

Dani squirmed in his arms, planting breathless kisses everywhere she could reach. Her response pushed him even higher, spiraling out of control until it was all he could do not to take her right here, right now.

"Carter," she whispered, her lips hot against his ear. "More."

More?

"I need you." Her hands slid beneath the waistband of his shorts. "Need you."

"Dani." He took her wrists in both his hands, holding her still. "Are you sure?"

"Mm-hmm." She tugged ineffectually at his grip, licked the whorl of his ear. "Very."

He shivered. "Um, okay, why don't we throw some clothes back on you, head over to my place..."

"No." This time, she bit his earlobe. "Here. Now."

Oh, God.

She tugged one hand free, slid it down inside his shorts, and curled around his...

He stepped back, gasping for air. She still gripped him, her hand sliding up and down his shaft with just the right amount of pressure. If she didn't stop now, he was going to come without her.

That would never do.

Drawing on the last of his reserves, he lifted her hand away, regretting the loss of her touch on his naked skin more than she'd ever know.

Naked skin.

Holy crap.

"Wait here," he ordered, his voice raspy with need. "I'll be right back."

Then, before she could protest, he took off out the door at a dead run.

Where was he going?

Dani shoved her hands through her hair, knowing there wasn't much she could do at this point that would mess it up more than it already was. It was tousled and snarled, like her worst case of bedhead ever.

Without the bed.

She groaned, letting her head drop down in frustration. One minute, she'd been living out her fantasy with Carter. The next, he was sprinting out the door like the hounds of hell were after him.

This was exactly what she'd been hoping to avoid when he'd suggested they go back to his place. No way was she giving him the opportunity to change his mind. Not when everything she'd ever dreamed about was actually about to come true.

But the longer he was out of this room, the likelier he was to come to his senses.

She caught a glimpse of herself in the mirror. A hot blush covered her from chest to eyebrows with the very visual reminder that she was still naked from the waist up. She anchored one arm across her breasts, managing to cover her tightly-beaded nipples at least, and pressed the other hand to her cheek. She looked tightly strung and highly aroused, a combination she feared would continue for the rest of the night.

This could have been her one chance to make love to the man she'd been in love with for years. But there was no way he'd still be interested by the time he got back from wherever he was.

"Hey."

She whirled around at the low, soft sound of his voice. "That was quick," she said, almost breathless with relief.

"Tell me about it." He kicked the door shut behind him, arms weighted down with a pile of white towels. "I think I set a land-speed record."

"So what did you—"

He dumped the towels on the ground in front of the mirrored wall and flashed her that devastating grin. "I thought the floor might be a little hard."

Before she even had enough time to process his comment, he was standing in front of her, gently moving her arm away from her chest so that she was exposed again.

The look in his eyes was hot and admiring, and she felt a rush of warmth between her legs in response.

"That's better." He glanced down at her feet. "Take off your shoes."

She toed them off, kicking each to the side before tugging off her socks as well. The polished wood floor was cool beneath her toes, a shivery contrast to the heat that coursed through her body.

Carter slid his hands up her arms, pausing at her shoulders to trace her collarbone with his thumbs. Goose bumps followed the path of his touch, causing a delicious shiver down her spine. He trailed his palms down her sides, pausing to cup the fullness of her breasts for a moment before continuing lower. Hooking his fingers in the sides of her workout shorts, he knelt and slid them down her legs to pool at her feet. He waited there, balancing her, as she stepped out of them. He'd managed to snag her panties, too, and she stood before him, completely naked, while he looked his fill.

And look he did, his gaze avid as he tilted his head back from his vantage point on his knees in front of her. His head was at waist-level, the perfect height for—

Dani clutched his head in her hands and groaned. He'd taken advantage of the situation and darted forward, swiping his tongue through her slick folds. His hands clasped her bottom, holding her steady, as he tasted her with leisurely strokes.

Her fingers clutched his hair, holding on for dear life as he licked her, swirling around her clitoris then back down to her aching core. Her breath came in panting little gasps, her hips starting to move in rhythmic counterpart to his sensual assault.

He gave one final lick, a long, tempting stroke that ended with a flick of the tongue against her clit that made her knees buckle. Laughing softly, he surged to his feet and lifted her into his arms.

"What are you doing?" She clutched his shoulders, a little impressed with her ability to form a complete sentence.

"Impressing you with my manly strength." He nipped at her earlobe. "Is it working?"

In response, she just laughed, wrapping her arms around him. He took a few steps over to the pile of towels and pretended to drop her. She shrieked, holding him even tighter, as he bent down and lowered her into the nest of white terrycloth.

She sucked in a breath. "Oh, my goodness."

He stretched out next to her. "Right out of the dryer," he boasted.

The freshly-laundered towels still retained most of the heat of the dryer, enveloping them both in a cocoon of warmth. Dani stretched out, enjoying the sensation of soft warm fabric against her naked skin.

"Keep doing that, and I won't be able to take it slowly," he warned.

"I don't want you to go slow," she said, amazed at her own boldness. "I want you to take me now."

He leaned over and pressed a hot, hard kiss to her lips. "Be careful what you wish for," he said, before stripping off the rest of his clothes.

She watched him as closely as he'd watched her, still not quite believing that she was getting naked with Carter. Part of her had always wondered if he'd live up to the hype of her personal fantasies.

Dani licked suddenly dry lips. Hell, yeah, he lived up to the hype.

His erection stood full and proud, the tip already glistening with pre-come. Her fingers twitched with the desire to touch him again, to feel that silky-smooth skin as she caressed him.

Skin.

Dani slapped a hand over her eyes and fell back into the towels. "I don't believe this," she groaned.

"Okay, not the reaction I was hoping for," Carter said.

She peeked at him between her fingers. "We can't...you know."

He swallowed. "Mind telling me why?"

"I don't make it a habit of carrying a condom to the gym with me."

He heaved a sigh of relief and fished a packet out from under the pile of towels. "Got it covered." Then he glanced down below the waist. "Well, not technically, but..."

Dani felt her jaw drop. "Okay, Houdini, wanna explain how you managed that little trick?"

Carter ripped the packet open and started to roll the condom on. "Actually, that's why I took off before. There's a condom machine in the men's room." He grinned at her. "The towels were just a bonus."

"Wow." She bit her lip, watching the slow slide of his fingers as he seated the condom. "I don't know what to say."

"How about, 'Come on down'?"

Laughing, she raised her arms to him. "Come here, Carter."

With a smile, he knelt between her legs, pressing her knees apart gently. She opened for him, groaning as he slid a finger inside.

"You are so ready," he said, eyes half-closed.

"I've been ready for years." Wincing, she watched for his reaction, but he only smiled absently, his attention diverted.

"I can't wait to be inside you." He looked at her intently. "Are you sure that's what you want, too?"

"Oh, Carter." She propped herself up on her elbows and kissed him. "More than anything in the world."

At that, he pressed forward, bracing his arms on either side of her waist. The thick head of his erection nudged against her, sliding slowly inside. He stopped, panting, teeth gritted.

Dani lifted her legs and pressed her heels into his buttocks. "All of you," she ground out, urging him forward. "I want all of you."

He surged forward, filling her completely, until he was seated to the hilt. They both groaned at the sensation. "Damn, you feel good," he said.

Dani clung to him as he pulled back, almost withdrawing, before sliding in again. Her shoulder blades pressed against the thick towels as she arched up to meet him. She felt stretched, full, taking more of him than she would have thought possible.

He slid his hands under her buttocks and tilted her up even further, angling her so that with each thrust he pressed against her clit. Bursts of pleasure echoed through her body, a spiral of desire so hot and thick she could almost taste it.

The music from the TV faded into the background as their panting breaths mingled and echoed through the empty room.

He looked down at her, his motions slowing. The expression on his face—a combination of heat and intensity—made her heart clench.

She was almost afraid to ask. "Carter?"

"You're amazing," he said. "And so damn hot."

Her breath left her lungs in a whoosh, relief washing through her. "I can live with that."

"I don't know. This may just be the death of me."

She laughed and slid her hands down his back, stroking the curve of his ass. "But what a way to go."

He growled and thrust into her again, pressing her back into the nest of towels. His gaze was captured by something over her shoulder, his expression growing even more intent.

"Carter?"

He tilted his head to the right. "Take a look."

She followed his gaze, eyes widening as she realized that they were in full, Technicolor splendor on the mirrored wall of the exercise room. She wrapped around him in a human version of yin and yang, her pale skin a striking contrast to his deep, golden tan.

"Yeah. So fuckin' hot."

Dani closed her eyes and arched into him, reveling in the feel of his heated skin against hers, the scatter of hair on his chest brushing against her taut nipples. Years of longing rose up in her, threatening to overwhelm her.

He leaned down and pressed kisses to her closed eyelids, her neck, as far down her chest as he could reach. He whispered hot suggestions in her ear, making her blush and bringing her to the edge of orgasm at the same time. Carter must have sensed it as well, because his thrusts grew wilder, more uncontrolled. They moved together in a rhythm that captured them both.

Dani tumbled first, crying out as waves of pleasure washed over her. Carter held her close as he thrust once, again, then a final time, collapsing with a shout on top of her.

Minutes ticked by, marked by the endless loop of the music of the menu screen on the DVD. Dani ducked her head into the curve of Carter's arm, willing the trembling to stop. He stroked her hair, isolating one strand to curl around his knuckle before finger-combing it back into place.

It should have been awkward. They'd taken their relationship from casual to over-the-top intimate in six-point-two seconds, without all the typical steps in between.

But all Dani could think, wrapped in Carter's arms, was that finally she was right where she was supposed to be.

Chapter Five

He woke up in an unfamiliar bed.

Despite his playboy reputation, this was not a common occurrence for Carter. Shifting uncomfortably under the floral sheets, he glanced across the pillows at the woman next to him.

He squeezed his eyes shut again.

What the hell had he done?

Dani rolled over in her sleep, arm flopping across his chest as she snuggled in. She took a deep, contented breath, burrowing even closer.

Carter stared up at the ceiling. Now he was trapped, literally, by the warm, lush body wrapped around him.

Despite his best intentions, his cock twitched at the thought. You would have thought he'd be out of commission for a while, after their marathon last night, but evidently his body had a mind of its own.

How many times had they made love? Three? Four?

Hell, he'd lost count after a while. And he couldn't even remember the last time that had happened.

He'd had the best intentions on the way home last night. It had been his turn to drive, so after the incident at the gym—that's what he was calling it, an incident—he'd given Dani a ride home. It had been a little awkward for both of them, considering they'd just gotten down and dirty in the aerobics room at the gym, but he'd been handling it well, all things considered. He would just drop her off with a kiss on the cheek, head back to his place for some serious alcohol therapy, and deal with it in the morning. Once he had a little perspective on the whole thing.

But when they got to Dani's place, she wasn't following the same script. No, she'd invited him in, eyes sexy and inviting, and then she'd placed her hand on his thigh.

His upper thigh.

Holy hell, she knew how to get to him.

So here he was, in his best friend's bed, wondering how long it would take before she started hating him.

Dani shifted again, snaking one leg over his waist, and he gritted his teeth. She was determined to kill him, wasn't she?

He was trying to be strong, trying to keep the mistakes of last night an isolated incident. If it just happened the one time—okay, four times—it would be easier to get their friendship back on track.

They could agree that they'd gotten this sexual attraction out of the way, and go on like it was before.

But how in the hell was he going to convince her of that if he got hard every time she touched him?

She shifted again, blinked her eyes, and turned a sleepy smile toward him. "Hey," she murmured.

"Morning." He shoved a hand through his hair. "How are you doing?"

"Fabulous." She traced a pattern on his bare chest. Shit. They were both naked, weren't they? "What about you?"

"Great."

This was going to be harder than he thought.

She lifted up on one elbow, hair tumbling around her bare shoulders. With a teasing smile, she leaned down and kissed him.

Her lips were soft and warm, and her naked breast brushed against his arm. That quickly, he wanted to roll her over and slip inside her, lose himself in the honeyed warmth of her body.

He had to stay strong. Had to. Their friendship depended on it.

Slowly she pulled back, eyes wary. "What's wrong?"

"Nothing's wrong," he said. But she scrambled to a sitting position, wrapping the sheet around her chest.

"Oh, my God," she said. "How did I miss it? It's written all over your face!"

Carter reached out to touch her—pat her shoulder, something—but she slapped his hand away.

"I wake up absolutely thrilled that you're finally in my bed, and you're trying to figure out how to get out of here without having to chew your own leg off."

"That's not the way it is, and you know it."

"Do I?" She glared at him. "Look me in the eye and tell me you're not regretting last night."

He opened his mouth. Closed it. "Dani, I—"

"Forget it." She scooted off the bed, taking the sheet with her. It dragged off Carter as well, leaving him naked on the bed. He grabbed a pillow and held it over his lap, but not quickly enough to hide the evidence of his arousal.

Dani gave him a withering glance. "Nice. So flattering." Her voice was sharp. "I'm going to the bathroom. Do us both a favor and be gone before I come out."

With that, she slammed the door behind her, leaving Carter alone in the room.

How long before she started hating him? Carter fell back on the bed, one arm flung over his eyes. Evidently, quicker than he'd ever anticipated.

Dani waited until she heard the front door to her apartment slam before she fell apart.

It had been touch and go there for a while, pretending to brush her teeth as she listened to him stomping around her bedroom on the other side of the bathroom door. From all the grumbling and mumbling going on, it was clear that he'd misplaced his underwear at some point last night.

Well, tough shit. If karma existed, he'd get chafe marks in unmentionable places.

Anger sustained her until she was sure he'd gone. Then, like a balloon suddenly losing air, she slid down onto the cold tile floor and started to cry.

Nothing dainty or feminine about it, either—great big heaving sobs, face mottled and tear-stained. Later, she hauled herself under the shower, turned the water on to high, and cried some more.

Somebody up there had a real sense of humor. She'd finally gotten what she'd dreamed of for so many years—the chance to be intimate with the man she loved. It had been the best night of her life.

But for Carter, it had obviously been the worst.

She'd often thought that being just friends with Carter was the hardest thing she'd ever done. But this was infinitely harder.

And it was going to get harder still.

She turned off the now-lukewarm shower and toweled off, padding into the bedroom in a daze. Though the room was deserted, Carter's uniquely masculine scent still lingered. Biting her lip, she headed for the closet. Blouse, slacks, suit jacket. Everything was done on auto-pilot, her mind still racing to the day ahead.

She had to be at OSE in half an hour.

And Carter would be there.

※

With luck, the sunglasses would provide some cover.

Carter headed into the building, head down, hoping against hope he could make it into his office without anyone noticing.

"Hey, boss-man!"

Damn. No such luck.

He turned and smiled briefly at the receptionist. "How are you today, Jessica?"

"Great!" She handed over a stack of paper. "Here's the end-of-quarter review."

"Thanks," he said, tucking it under his arm. "I'll take a look at it later."

"Oh, and Dani wanted me to let you know that she'll have the financial report to you by noon," Jess continued.

Oh, hell. It was worse than he'd thought. They were reduced to passing messages through the receptionist.

In the eight years they'd worked together, Dani had never relied on the grapevine. She'd always talked directly to him.

Damn, he was in trouble.

"Thanks," he said again, since he couldn't think of a single other thing to say. Then he turned back and added, "Hold my calls, please."

"Sure thing." She laughed. "I'm starting to think that's the catchphrase of the day."

"What do you mean?"

"You're the second person to ask me to hold their calls today. Dani's locked up tight in her office, too. If you're not careful, I'll start to think there's a conspiracy."

He gave her a half-hearted wave and headed for his office, the beginnings of a migraine banding his head.

Oh, there was a conspiracy all right. But it was directed at him.

And the hell of it was, he deserved it.

༄༅

If he apologized, she was going to kill him.

Taking a deep breath, Dani opened the door to Carter's office and walked inside. He was standing opposite his desk, looking out the floor to ceiling windows at the view of downtown Seattle. The Sound was visible beyond the high-rise buildings, gunmetal gray under the clouds.

He turned as she entered, his hands tucked in his pockets. "Hey," he said softly, a smile curving his lips. Almost immediately, he bit it back, pasting a look of concern on his face that set her nerves on edge. "How are you?"

"I told you. I'm fine." She knew he was having a hard time with this, but dammit, so was she. Why would fate be so cruel as to give her her heart's desire, and then snatch it away again?

"Good." He sat on the edge of his desk, one foot swinging idly. "I'm glad."

Oh, God. It was even worse than she'd anticipated. They'd been reduced to meaningless platitudes.

Turning, she walked over to the door and shut it firmly. "Okay, Carter, here's how it is." She ignored his double-take and charged ahead. "Last night, we had sex."

"Uh..."

"And I don't regret a minute of it. We're both young, single—" She stopped abruptly. "Shit. Tell me you aren't seeing anyone."

"Of course not."

She took a deep breath. "Good."

"I wouldn't do that." He looked hurt. "You know me better than that."

"You're right. I do know you better than that." She paused for effect. "And you know me."

He nodded.

"So you know that I'd never let anyone take advantage of me. Even you."

"I never said—"

"You didn't have to say. It's in everything you haven't said, the way you're tiptoeing around me like I've got some terminal disease and you don't want to be the one who has to break the news. What happened isn't a tragedy. So just stop it, okay? No regrets. No apologies."

"Okay. Friends?" He stuck out his hand, waiting to shake on it.

"Of course." A shiver of awareness traveled through her as their palms touched, a vivid reminder of the night before. "Under the circumstances, though, it would probably be better if we stopped the after-hours workouts."

He nodded once. Gaze fixed out the window, he said, "And it's fine if you drop out of the Challenge, too."

"Why would I drop out of the Challenge?"

"I just meant that if you couldn't find another class that worked with your schedule…"

"Wait." She held up her hand. "Who said anything about another class?"

"You're not seriously thinking of staying in a strip aerobics class, are you?"

She crossed her arms over her chest. "I most certainly am."

He stared at her, mouth open. "You're going to keep taking your clothes off? In public?"

Dani raised an eyebrow. "What I choose to do in my personal time is none of your business, Carter."

"I just don't see how it's appropriate for you to—"

"Give me a break." She glared at him. "If you think I'm going to run around stripping for every guy I meet, you don't know me at all. This is an aerobics class, with a little bit of attitude. I like it. I'm good at it. And nobody, least of all you, has the right to dictate whether I can stay in it or not."

He spluttered a little, but she held out a hand. "Forget it, Carter. Your objection has been noted. Let's just leave it at that."

Before he could say anything, she walked to the door. Then she left his office, shutting the door behind her.

ಬಿಲ್

"I am so jealous." Jessica handed Dani a manila envelope. "You are going to have such a great time."

"Excuse me?" Dani opened the envelope and slid the contents onto her desk. One looked suspiciously like a plane ticket.

"Going to Vegas for the trade show this weekend. Don't tell me you forgot!" Jessica shook her head. "Girl, you'd forget your head if it wasn't stapled on."

Dani frowned. "I didn't forget." Damned if she hadn't avoided thinking about it, though.

"Two nights in Vegas with the boss-man." Jessica fanned herself. "Don't do anything I wouldn't do."

That didn't leave Dani with a lot of options. "No worries," she said. Even if she wanted it, Carter had made it very clear he wasn't going there again.

"Are you kidding? Just pack a few of those hot new outfits you've been wearing and he'll be all over you."

Hot new...? Dani blushed. "I don't think so."

"Seriously. He won't be able to resist."

Resisting wasn't the problem. Regretting it afterward was. "Workplace romances are a bad idea," Dani said.

Jessica, undaunted, winked at her. "Remember, what happens in Vegas..."

"Is none of anyone else's business." Carter strolled into the room and picked up Dani's plane ticket.

Jessica pushed out her lower lip. "You two are no fun. Can I at least make up some rumors to spread?"

Carter shrugged and sat on the edge of Dani's desk. "Knock yourself out."

Dani watched Jessica leave the room. "Nobody would believe it anyway," she muttered.

"What was that?"

Dani shook her head. "Never mind." She snatched the plane ticket out of his hand. "We leave Friday morning?"

"Crack of dawn." He glanced at the open door to her office and lowered his voice. "Dani, are you okay with this?"

She shot him a glance. "Why wouldn't I be?"

"Dani..."

"Don't worry." She held up a hand. "I'll do my best to keep from throwing myself at you."

"That's not what I meant and you know it."

She sighed. "Carter, we're going to Las Vegas for work, and that's the one thing I know I'm good at. So you can rest easy. I'll be the consummate professional. Now, if you'll excuse me, I have some work to do."

He shook his head and stalked out the door. Dani watched him go.

Jessica had it backwards. The gossip-worthy stuff had happened right here.

It was Vegas that was going to be one long, excruciating nothing.

ඞඥ

Carter shifted in his seat and checked his watch for the umpteen millionth time.

Where the hell was she?

"Can I get you something, sir?" The flight attendant hovered over him, a concerned expression on her face. "A pillow, something to drink?"

He shook his head. All he wanted was Dani.

Here. He wanted her here, on the plane, on time. He didn't *want* her, want her.

Maybe if he kept telling himself that, it'd be true.

"Sorry I'm late." Dani dropped down into the seat next to him, her hair tousled and her face pink with exertion. "The tram to this part of the terminal broke down and I had to hoof it."

Carter glanced at her and looked away quickly so he wouldn't be tempted to stare. Damn, she looked good. Her sea green, long-sleeve shirt had a scoop neckline, and her cleavage rose and fell as she caught her breath.

Ah, hell. Did he have to notice her cleavage?

He blew out a frustrated breath and tried to think of something else.

No, it was no use. All his attention was riveted on the woman sitting far too close to him.

"First class?" She raised an eyebrow. "Honestly, Carter, are you ever going to stick to a budget?"

"I am," he shot back. "I upgraded from coach with my frequent flier miles."

"For both of us?" She smiled at him for the first time in what seemed like weeks. "That was very nice of you."

He didn't want to be nice. He wanted to blow off the conference and spend the entire time in bed with Dani. He wanted to strip her naked and keep her that way until he'd sated his hunger for her. He wanted to drag her off to the back of the plane and join the Mile High Club before they even reached the city of sin.

But doing any of those things would be the death knell of his friendship with Dani. He needed her in his life far more than he needed to slake his lust. Again.

Friendship lasted. Relationships never did.

Friendship.

Focus on the friendship.

Dani cleared her throat. Carter looked up and realized that he'd been lost in thought long enough to be rude. "Did you really think I'd leave you back in coach while I enjoyed first class? Damn, woman, you'd kick my ass."

"No, I'd congratulate you on being frugal." She laughed, a rich throaty sound that made him shift uncomfortably in his seat. "*Then* I'd kick your ass."

They were both silent for a while, which didn't bother Carter nearly as much as it did with other women. But then, most women weren't Dani.

How could he have been so selfish as to jeopardize their friendship for a roll in the sack?

Her hair, pinned on top of her head in a haphazard knot, managed to look sexy and sweetly goofy at the same time. A few little tendrils drifted around her face and neck. His fingers itched to touch them.

Carter sighed and took the flute of champagne the flight attendant was holding out. He had a feeling he was going to need it.

Chapter Six

Carter stood next to the wall, nursing a shot of single malt. The conference room had been transformed by the casino staff into a private reception hall, with a half-dozen bartending stations and two long buffet tables down each side of the room. It was teeming with conference-goers enjoying the extravagant buffet and open bar, as well as the chance to network.

Schmooze. And he just was not in the mood for it tonight.

It was crazy. This was the whole reason he'd come to the conference—talking up OSE, meeting people who could help expand their markets and bring their products to a national stage. So why was he standing here in the shadows, the epitome of anti-social?

"Nice presentation today, Matthews," a voice boomed next to him. "You and your partner did an excellent job introducing your products."

Carter turned to see Jack Madison, buyer for a national sporting goods chain, standing beside him. "I'm glad you liked it," he said.

"Absolutely." Jack flung an arm around his shoulder and steered him into the room. "In fact, I'd like the chance to discuss your prospects more in-depth, if you don't mind."

Carter did mind; he'd rather ditch the party and head back to his room to sulk. Over what, he had no idea. And he knew that giving in to his snit would be an incredibly stupid thing to do.

So, instead, he agreed to join Jack at a table across the room. Once there, a few more buyers joined them, as well as an investor who had been making some noises about helping OSE find a wider customer base. Soon, Carter was deep in conversation, almost able to ignore his bad mood.

Until Jack leaned over and said, "And there's one of your best assets."

Carter followed his gaze to the entryway to the room, and his mood plummeted. What the hell was she doing here?

Deep down, he knew he was being unreasonable. She had every right to be here, just like every other attendee. In fact, it would look strange if she didn't attend the biggest social event of the conference.

But damn, did she have to look so good?

She stood just inside the doorway, her hair tumbling around her shoulders in a mass of curls. A white sleeveless sweater hugged her curves, while her flirty red skirt ended well above her knees. She looked sexy and approachable at the same time.

Carter clenched his jaw so hard he was at risk of breaking a tooth.

She saw him then, and the smile that lit her face warmed a place deep inside that he couldn't even name. She wove her way through the crowd, making small talk with the other attendees, until she reached the table. "Mind if I join you?"

Almost instantaneously, the other men at the table jumped to their feet, holding out a chair for her, offering to fetch a drink, complimenting her on her outfit. Carter rose as well, holding back a glower with effort.

"Loved your budget rundown this afternoon," Fred said. The heavyset, balding man was one of the top decision-makers for an east coast department store chain that was looking to expand into outdoor gear. He pushed the platter of appetizers toward Dani. "You've got a real handle on money issues."

"That's her specialty," Carter couldn't help saying. "No one's better at finance than Dani."

"Thanks, Carter." Dani smiled at him. "I do my best."

"What else are you good at, Dani?" Jack leaned forward, one arm on the table.

"I—I don't know," she stammered. "I'm pretty focused on my work."

"How about dancing?" Jack gestured toward the dance floor at the far end of the room. "Care to take a spin with me?"

Carter smiled inwardly. Jack was about to get his head handed to him. Dani never danced with anyone.

His mouth dropped open as Dani smiled up at Jack and placed her hand in his.

The two of them headed for the dance floor and found a spot. It was like a train wreck—Carter simply couldn't look away. They were closer than should be legal, Jack's hand hovering too damn close to Dani's ass. And what the hell was Dani doing? That hip-wiggle thing?

Then he recognized it. It was the same move she'd been doing in the aerobics room the night he'd walked in on her erotic strip tease.

His jaw tightened and he clenched his hands as Dani and Jack burned up the dance floor. It was—obscene, that's what it was.

"Damn," Fred said as he swallowed the last of his beer. "That is one hot woman."

Carter whipped his head around. "Who?"

Fred gestured at the dance floor with his empty bottle. "Your financial officer. Who'd have guessed she'd have a booty like that?"

"Excuse me?"

Fred, oblivious, chattered on. "I wouldn't mind getting to know her better. Is she seeing anyone right now?"

"What?"

"Of course, you know what they say...what happens in Vegas..." Fred winked at him.

Carter leaned forward, eyes narrowed. "I'd better not hear you say anything like that again."

Fred held up his hands. "Whoa, man, just making an observation."

"A pretty disrespectful one," Carter growled.

"Didn't realize that the two of you had a thing. Sorry."

"We don't have a thing," Carter said. He crossed his arms over his chest. "I just don't like hearing a colleague talked about that rudely."

"Sure." Fred stood and looked around. "Think I'll go, uh, get another drink."

Carter turned back toward the dance floor, where the music had segued into a slow song. Jack was sticking to Dani like Cling Wrap. Slamming his glass down on the table, Carter jumped to his feet. He knew he was being unreasonable—not to mention totally obvious—but he couldn't seem to help himself.

Carter stalked over to the dance floor, his face hot with anger. Barely hanging on to his civility by a thread, he tapped Jack on the shoulder.

Jack turned around, an amused expression on his face. "Did you need something?"

"I need to talk to Dani, if you don't mind."

"In the middle of a song?" At Carter's glower, he stepped back from Dani, hands raised. "Sorry, man. All yours."

Damn straight. Carter took Dani's hand and pulled her into his arms, holding her a respectable distance apart. His body urged him to hold her closer, but he wasn't going there. No matter how much he wanted it.

Dani, however, didn't seem to want it at all. "What the heck are you doing? That was embarrassing," she hissed.

"As embarrassing as all the dirty dancing you and Jack were up to?"

She pulled back, glaring at him. "I don't believe you."

"You were all over each other."

"We were *dancing*. It's normal behavior on the dance floor."

"Please. You couldn't have gotten any closer without removing articles of clothing."

"I think you need to stop now, Carter."

She was right, but he plowed on, too angry to censor himself. "And you sure know something about taking your clothes off, don't you?"

Furious, she wrenched herself from his arms and stalked off the dance floor, heading for the back hallway. Carter followed a few steps behind.

She paused at the door of the women's restroom and, holding a hand out, stiff-armed to stop him from going any further. "Go away, Carter. I can't be around you when you're like this."

"Like what?" He captured her hand against his chest, pulled her close. "Jealous as hell?"

"Jealous?" She swallowed, eyes wide. "What are you talking about?"

"This." And the noise and commotion of the bar faded into nothingness as he lowered his head for a kiss.

There was nothing hesitant about it, a brazen mating of lips and tongues that sent him up in flames. The pent-up frustration of the past week, knowing what it was like to touch her and being unable to do anything about it, finally dissolved in a flurry of passionate kisses.

One hand cupped the back of her head, holding it steady as his lips plundered hers. The other slid down her back, dipping to the sweet curve of her ass.

With a helpless moan, Dani grabbed the lapel of his shirt and hauled him even closer, opening her mouth to his. Carter stroked his tongue inside, sampling the sharp bite of the wine she'd been drinking as it mingled with the heady flavor of Dani.

She whimpered against his mouth, pressing her mound into his erection with little pulsing movements.

Another step closer and he had her back against the wall, one leg wrapped around his. He braced his hands on either side of her head and broke the kiss, lifting up briefly to look at her.

Her chest rose and fell with each panting breath, her pulse beating rapidly in the hollow of her throat. She dropped her head back against the wall with an audible thud, eyes closed, as he planted featherlight kisses down the column of her neck.

He pushed up the hem of her fitted shirt, burrowing his hand underneath to touch the heated skin of her midriff. She sucked in a breath, inadvertently giving him greater access to her torso. He traced a finger along the band of her bra, knuckles skimming the lace-covered swell of her breasts. They both groaned at the contact.

Damn, he was hard, and growing harder by the second. Her leg was still wrapped around his waist, her skimpy red skirt riding dangerously high up her thigh. One tug at the thin fabric and her undies would be visible to the world.

Undies that, if he didn't miss his guess, were already damp.

He stroked his hand higher, brushing his thumb across one taut nipple. Dani whimpered and laced her fingers through his hair, tugging his head up for another kiss. Her hips pressed against his, bringing her into perfect alignment with his erection.

Lower the zipper, pull aside the scrap of satin covering her mound, and he could be inside her right here, right now.

In the back hallway of the casino, where anyone could walk by at any minute.

Hell, maybe they already had. He was so caught up in the moment a damn marching band could have thundered by and he would have missed it.

Shaken by his lack of control, Carter pushed away from the wall and, by extension, away from Dani. Whirling around, he paced across the hallway and turned back.

Her clothing was askew, her hair mussed and wild. She tucked her shirt in with trembling hands.

"Dani, I—"

"Stop." She looked him in the eye. "I'm going back to the table. I'm going to get my purse, say goodbye to everyone, and leave. I'd appreciate it if you could give me five minutes before you come back." She turned to go, then looked at him over her shoulder. "I'll be in my room in ten minutes. Knock on the adjoining door if you're interested in continuing this."

It took Carter the full ten minutes—and then some—to decide what, exactly, he was going to do.

༄༅

Dani paced her hotel room from door to window and back again.

Was she crazy, or what?

She pressed a hand to her stomach, her nerves tumbling around like socks in a dryer. Any minute now, Carter was going to knock on the door between their rooms.

Or not.

She glanced at the connecting door, wondering which scared her more—the idea that Carter might take her up on her offer, or the thought that he'd turn her down.

And why was she coming back for more emotional punishment? The last week had been hell at work, with the two of them avoiding each other as much as possible. She'd even taken to sending him her reports via e-mail, instead of dropping them off at his office on her way somewhere else. She'd stopped inventing reasons to run into him during the day, because the awkwardness between them was too painful.

It was almost like they didn't work together anymore.

Strange as it seemed, some of that had disappeared on the flight to Vegas.

As much as she'd been dreading this business trip, they'd actually seemed to find a way back to their friendship.

Up until tonight.

Carter had been an absolute bear, glaring and barking at everyone in his path, until she'd been certain he'd blown whatever chance they had to expand OSE's reach beyond the Northwest. Talk about burning bridges. She'd been thrilled to have a chance to escape to the dance floor with Jack.

And just when she'd softened him up, convinced him to take OSE's info packet back to headquarters and talk them up to his supervisors, Carter had to show up like some overbearing Neanderthal and whisk her away.

She could only hope her hard work hadn't been in vain.

She checked her watch again, stomach clenching. He should have been here by now.

Maybe his fancy talk about jealousy had been so much hot air. Maybe that kiss hadn't meant anything more to him than a casual peck on the cheek.

He had a well-deserved reputation as a playboy. A new woman every month, each more stunning than the one before. What did she have to offer a man like that?

Only her heart. And she was so afraid that just wouldn't be enough.

He wasn't coming. He'd come to his senses, realized that if they made love again, it would make things just that more complicated. He was probably still down at the reception, drinking a beer with the guys and thanking his lucky stars he'd escaped with his sanity.

She never should have...

The doorknob turned.

Carter was beyond finesse.

Three strides took him across the room to where Dani stood. Without a word, he took her hand, and led her to the bedroom.

He turned on the bedside lamp and sat on the bed. "Dance for me," he said.

"What?" Her voice was barely above a whisper.

"I want to see what you've learned in this class of yours. I want you to know that I'm watching this time." He leaned back against the headboard. "I want to know you're dancing just for me."

"I don't have any music," she protested. Her breathing accelerated and her pupils dilated. "I'll look silly."

"No, you won't." Feeling reckless, he added, "Strip for me, Dani."

She closed her eyes. Maybe he'd pushed too far, asked too much. She was going to tell him to get out, to forget the whole thing...

She began to sway back and forth, following an internal beat. She stroked her hands up her sides and into her hair, lifting it off her neck. Then she tilted her head back, swinging the thick brown curls from side to side. Her breasts tilted up, the tight nipples clearly visible through the thin fabric of her top.

She did that little hip-shimmy, the one he'd seen on the dance floor, and Carter sucked in a breath. He could see a wicked smile curve her lips before she turned around and did the same shimmy facing away from him.

His cock was aching, thick and hard behind the fly of his pants. He slid the zipper down, and the sound was startlingly loud in the silent bedroom.

Dani froze for just a moment, but started to move again right away, her dancing growing bolder and more erotic. Still facing away from him, she put her hands in the small of her back and slid them down, cupping her ass. One hand teased the hem of her skirt, drawing it up just far enough to give him a peek-a-boo view of her thigh-high stockings.

Carter groaned.

She lowered the skirt again and gave her left cheek a little slap.

Not taking his eyes off her, Carter slid his pants off, dropping them over the side of the bed.

Dani looked over her shoulder at him and smiled. Then she criss-crossed her arms in front of her, grasped the hem of her shirt, and in one smooth movement pulled it off.

She turned around, her white lace bra barely covering her nipples. She ran a finger along the edges, dipping into the valley between her breasts and back up again. Swaying back and forth, she slipped her hands into the waistband of her skirt and stripped it all the way off.

Carter yanked his shirt off. He was in just his boxers now, his hard-on clearly outlined by the thin fabric. With one hand, he released it and began to stroke, eyes still focused on her.

Dani licked her lips, watching him avidly. She hooked a finger in one bra strap and drew it down her arm, following suit with the other. A flick of the front closure and her breasts swung free, the bra joining her other clothing on the floor.

She was almost naked now, just a barely-there thong and those thigh-high stockings. He crooked a finger at her, still stroking himself.

She crawled up onto the bed, her hair brushing his thighs as she moved toward him.

Her face was just above his, her eyes bright and vivid. Leaning down, she kissed him, her hand replacing his on his cock.

He arched up as she stroked him from root to tip, her thumb spreading the glistening liquid around the swollen head. He slipped her thong to the side. She was wet and ready for him. Not bothering to finish undressing her, he aligned his cock with her opening and slid inside.

He groaned as she took all of him, pressing down until he was fully seated inside her.

Dani lifted up until just the tip of him was in her. Closing her eyes, she began to ride him.

He reached between them and found her clit, pressing gently against it as she moved. Then he raised his head and took one nipple into his mouth.

Dani gasped at the dual assault, her movements growing wilder and more uncontrolled. Carter gripped her hips and began to thrust, powering them both to the edge.

Suddenly, Dani stiffened, her muscles trembling as wave after wave of pleasure washed over her. Carter gritted his teeth against the sensation of her inner muscles pulsing around him. Only after she slumped against him, boneless, did he let his orgasm rip through him.

They lay together for long minutes, struggling to get their breathing under control. Finally, he rolled to the side, sliding out of her—

And swore when he realized there was no condom to dispose of.

"What is it?" Dani rose up on one elbow.

He covered his eyes with one hand. "I can't believe I forgot birth control," he said.

"Oh. That." She shrugged. "I took care of it before you got here."

"What?" He glanced at her.

"There are other methods of birth control, you know."

"But I never forget the condom." What had he been thinking?

He hadn't been thinking. That was the problem.

"I know," she said. "I didn't expect we'd forget tonight, either. But no method is a hundred percent safe, so I figured a backup wouldn't hurt." She laughed softly. "Glad I planned ahead."

He didn't feel like laughing. How could he have been so irresponsible?

"Dani, I'm so sorry," he said.

"Why?" She scooted up on the bed, unconcerned with her nudity. "It's not your fault."

"Yes, it is. All of it."

Her eyes narrowed. "What do you mean, all of it?"

"I should have stayed away."

"Don't." She held up a hand, not looking at him. "I don't want to hear it."

"It's just that I—"

"You're sorry. Again. You regret what you just did. Again." She shoved a hand through her hair, working out the worst of the snarls with her fingers. "Want to know what I regret? Letting myself get caught up in the moment with you. Because when you start beating yourself up over *our* actions, I'm the one who gets bruised."

Dani got up and walked to the bathroom, grabbing her robe from the hook on the wall. She came back in, tying the belt around her. "I can't do this anymore, Carter. I can't be some dirty little secret, good only for a quick grope followed by days of self-flagellation. You have to figure out what you want. See, I already know what I want. And it isn't this."

Carter sat back, gutted. "Dani," he said.

She shook her head. "No more, Carter. I have to respect myself more than that."

Then she reached down, handed him his clothing, and stalked out of the room.

Chapter Seven

Jessica was on the phone when Dani arrived at work Monday.

It was about the only thing that had gone right that morning.

No, scratch that. It was the only thing that had gone right since her first night in Vegas.

She slipped past the reception desk and into her office, shutting the door tightly behind her.

She didn't want to see anyone, didn't want to have to answer all the inevitable questions about the trip. What in the world was she supposed to say? *Yeah, it was great until I slept with Carter and we ended up not speaking to each other for the rest of the conference?*

Which was pretty impressive, actually, when you considered just how many activities they were required to attend together.

And even when the conference was over and they were on their way home, the tension between them was oppressively thick. Every now and then she'd catch Carter giving her that "just-kicked-puppy-dog" look, like he was the one who'd had his heart ripped out and left bleeding on the floor. By the time the plane landed at Sea-Tac, Dani was ready to scream.

Home wasn't any better. Her empty apartment was another reminder of what she wanted and couldn't have. The dread in the pit of her stomach at the thought of going to work with Carter every day from here on out was enough to keep her awake half the night.

The cold, empty feeling at the thought of leaving OSE so she wouldn't have to be around him every day was enough to ruin the other half.

She'd tossed and turned, finally falling asleep somewhere between two a.m. and dawn, only to discover on awakening that she'd forgotten to set her alarm. She'd still only gotten a few hours of sleep, but was now an hour and a half late for work. Cursing roundly, she'd jumped into the shower to find that the hot water heater had given up the ghost sometime during her absence. Shivering, exhausted, she'd gotten dressed and rushed out the door.

Halfway to OSE she'd realized that she'd left her briefcase on the kitchen counter.

On the bright side, at least I-5 wasn't as crowded this hour of the morning.

She powered up her computer, kicked off her shoes—one black, one navy, she noted with a grimace—and settled back to dig her way through four days of e-mail.

She scrolled through the list, quickly deleting all junk mail and companywide messages that didn't relate to her. Near the bottom of the page one of the messages had a red flag next to it.

Her stomach dove when she saw who'd sent it.

Carter.

Gritting her teeth, she clicked on it. Better to get it over with quickly, like pulling off a band-aid.

It was short to the point of terseness. *We need to talk.*

She hit reply. *I'm pretty busy today.*

This time, an instant message dinged, startling her. Her stomach twisted at the thought of him sitting at his desk, waiting for her reply. *Make time.*

She leaned back, eyes narrowed. She could ignore him, but it was a sure bet that if she did, he'd be knocking down her door in a matter of minutes.

Better not to create a scene. *Fine. When and where?*

I'll let you know. And with that, he signed off.

Dani stared at the computer screen, wondering how in the world she was supposed to get any work done after that.

ഌ෬

Dani filed the last of the reports away, glancing out her window at the glow on Puget Sound from the setting sun. The stack of paperwork that had been waiting on her desk when she got back from Vegas had disappeared, but if someone had asked what they'd been about, she'd have been hard pressed to answer. The numbers had flowed together in one big amorphous mess as she powered through the pages, too distracted to really concentrate.

Carter had never gotten back to her.

He'd make a great torturer, she fumed as she checked her e-mail one last time. Leaving her hanging like that was killing her.

Nope, no messages. She shut down the computer and grabbed her purse, stomach growling with the reminder that she hadn't eaten all day. She'd pick up dinner on the way home, hope the super had fixed the water heater so she could soak in a hot tub, and forget she'd ever known Carter Matthews.

She opened the door, not surprised that the office was empty. She'd worked later tonight than she had in a long time, waiting for the other shoe to drop.

Dani turned to close the door and was startled to find an envelope taped to it. Inside was a single note card, with Carter's distinctive handwriting on it. *Second floor. 8 p.m.*

She scowled at the note. She had less than five minutes to make it on time. Trust Carter to make a production out of this.

She got off the elevator on the second floor, only to find the health club closed up tight and another envelope taped to the door. She tipped a key into her palm. This note said: *Come in. Check the front desk.*

A little nervous, she unlocked the door and slipped inside. A card propped on the counter read: *Follow the red ribbon.*

The ribbon trailed along the floor, leading past the treadmills and free weights, beyond the racquetball courts and down the hall to the aerobics room. A bright red bow decorated the door.

Taking a deep breath, she pressed a hand to her stomach in a futile attempt to calm her nerves. Turning the knob, she stepped inside.

The room had been transformed. She took a few steps in, turning around to try to take it all in. A round table sat in the middle of the room, covered with a white linen tablecloth. It was set for one.

In front of the table, backed up against the wall of mirrors, a stage had been erected. It was a couple of feet off the ground, and lights shone on it from metal stands on either side.

Right smack dab in the center was—a pole?

"Good evening," Carter said, in a rough approximation of a waiter at a formal restaurant. Either that or Herman Munster. He was standing near the back, a towel draped across one arm. "Welcome to Carter's."

"What in the world?" Dani's legs felt suddenly weak, and she fumbled for the chair. In a flash, he was across the room, holding it out for her.

"I'm sorry, ma'am, but questions will have to wait." When she was seated, he returned to the back of the room and wheeled over a cart filled with covered dishes. "Your dinner."

She stared as he whipped off the cover of one of the dishes to reveal a full steak dinner. "How did you—"

"Shh." He placed a finger against her lips. "No questions. Just eat."

Shooting him a dubious look, she put her napkin in her lap. At the first bite, she moaned with delight. The steak was cooked to perfection, tender and juicy. Unable to hold back, she tucked into the meal. She looked up to see Carter standing at her elbow, waiting patiently. "Aren't you eating?"

He just smiled and shook his head, gesturing at her to continue.

She shrugged and kept eating. Finally, she pushed the plate away with a sigh.

He skimmed the plate off her table, replacing it with a smaller one. Under this cover was a chocolate torte, a rich berry sauce drizzled over it.

"I think you've just killed the Wellness Challenge for me," she said with a laugh.

He crouched down next to the table to look her in the eye. "You don't need it." Then he stood and walked over to the side of the stage.

Carter leaned down and fiddled with the stereo system. With a click, the soft instrumental music that had been playing stopped, only to be replaced by a sensual, beat-driven melody. Dani stopped eating, fork halfway to her mouth, as Carter jumped up onto the stage.

"And now for the entertainment portion of our evening." He took the towel off his arm and tossed it offstage.

Dani could only watch, mouth gaping, as Carter began to dance. He swiveled his hips to the beat, toying with the top button on his shirt. One by one, he slid the buttons free, until the white dress shirt hung open, revealing a slice of skin that made Dani's mouth water more than the chocolate had. The music crescendoed, and a half-beat later, he stripped off the shirt, stopping again as he got caught in the still-buttoned cuffs. "Damn!"

Dani stifled a giggle as he struggled his way out of the sleeves. Then the shirt was gone, tossed to the side, and she was too busy admiring his chest to laugh.

With one hand, he grasped the pole, swinging around from one side to the other. Dani supposed it was meant to look like a pole dance at a strip club, but in Carter's hands it was closer to rappelling up a rock wall. He did a little bump and grind to the music, his black slacks incongruously formal against the blatantly sexual setting.

It was both funny and sensual, and Dani sat with her hand over her mouth, dessert forgotten, as her favorite treat made a very sexy fool out of himself just for her.

He reached for his belt buckle, whipping the belt out of the loops so quickly he had to duck to avoid smacking himself in the face with it. Dropping it to the ground with a curse, he fumbled with the button on his slacks, slipping them to the floor only to get tangled in his shoes.

"Ah, hell." He stopped dancing and stood in the middle of the stage, pants around his ankles, clad only in a pair of boxer short. He spread his arms wide and looked at her, a hesitant smile on his face. "Surprise."

"Carter, you goofball." Dani bit her lip to keep from crying. "What the hell are you doing?"

He shuffled over to the CD player and switched it off. Then he sat on the edge of the stage, still partially dressed. "I think I'm apologizing."

"For what?" She sat ramrod-straight in her chair, fighting the urge to go to him. She just couldn't, not yet.

"For screwing everything up." He leaned back, unselfconsciously, and rested his palms on the floor behind him. "I was so afraid of ruining the best relationship I'd ever had, I didn't take the time to notice that the only thing damaging it was my own attitude."

"What do you mean?" Her voice trembled a little.

"You're my best friend, Dani." He looked at her, eyes intent. "But I haven't been acting like it lately. I've never had a relationship last more than a few months, so I decided a relationship with you would suffer the same fate. I didn't want that to happen."

"I didn't, either."

"So I pushed you away, trying to deny what was happening between us."

She took a deep breath. "What is happening between us?"

He hopped off the stage and shuffled over to her, his pants still caught around his ankles. It should have been funny, but Dani felt about as far from laughing as possible. "I've fallen in love with you," he said, cupping her face in his hand.

"I thought I wasn't your type," she whispered, leaning into his touch.

"My type?"

"Glamorous, sexy, athletic."

He laughed softly. "Are you kidding?" He pulled her to her feet and wrapped his arms around her, his hard-on pressing against her stomach. "Have you looked in a mirror lately?"

She glanced at the mirrored wall, their reflection large as life. She blinked in surprise. She did look different—her hair was down, soft curls framing her face. Her sweater and khaki pants were closer-fitting than what she'd worn before the challenge, hugging every curve.

"Why do you think I've had such a hard time keeping my hands off you?" He palmed her hip. "God, you turn me on."

"I thought you were ashamed of me," she said.

"Never." He shook his head. "Ashamed of myself, for risking the most important relationship in my life by giving in to my attraction to you. I thought that when it ended, I'd lose you for good."

"No."

"I know that now. Just like I know it doesn't have to end."

"What do you mean?"

"I mean that I love you, Dani. I want to be with you now and always, as a friend, as a lover, as a partner. Forever." He reached down and patted his hip, grimacing as he realized that his pocket was on the floor with the rest of his pants. "Maybe I ought to get dressed again for this," he muttered.

"No way." She gave him a fierce hug. "I think I want to keep you just like this."

"Half-naked?"

"In more ways than one." She smiled shyly. "You love me?"

He nodded. "Everything about you. I love how you get so immersed in your work you lose track of time. I love how you're willing to try new things, even when they're outside your comfort zone. I love that you're a great friend and an even better lover. I even love how you try to keep me to a budget. I love you, Dani Williams."

Her eyes welled with tears. "I love you, too, Carter. I've loved you forever."

"Thank God." He crushed her to him, her curves molding to his angles. "Now I really do need my pants."

She laughed, brushing away a tear as he stepped away. "I never thought I'd hear those words from you."

"What, that I need my pants?" He hitched them up, letting them hang loosely on his hips.

"That, too." She watched him dig around in his pocket. "What are you doing?"

He pulled out a small drawstring velvet bag. "Getting this."

Her eyes widened as he opened the bag and tipped out something sparkly.

He took the ring between thumb and forefinger and held it out to her. "How would you feel about making this partnership permanent?"

Her hand shook only a little as she stretched it toward him. "I think it's a fine idea," she said.

Carter slid the ring on; it fit perfectly. "So how tight a budget are we going to be on for the wedding?"

Dani grinned. "Budget? Are you kidding? I'm only ever getting married once. We're going to do it up right."

"Good." He sat on the edge of the makeshift stage and tugged her down next to him. "Let's consider tonight one of the expenses, okay? You don't want to know how much this cost."

"I think you're right." She looked around. "How in the world did you manage to set this up, anyway?"

"I have my ways." He wrapped an arm around her shoulder. "It was convincing them to close up a couple of hours early that took the most doing."

"Wow." She leaned against him, her head on his shoulder. "I can't believe you went to all this trouble."

He kissed her forehead. "You're worth it."

"I do have one question." She glanced over her shoulder. "What's with the pole?"

"Well, I figured since you've done so well with strip aerobics…"

Dani blushed. "Carter."

"Why not take the class to the next level?"

"Are you telling me this is my very own pole?"

"Our pole," he corrected, a gleam in his eye. "Sturdy yet portable."

"I like the way you think," she teased.

"Besides, I've got a vested interest in helping you win the Wellness Challenge."

"You do?"

He waggled his eyebrows. "I'm thinking that trip to Hawaii would be an excellent honeymoon trip."

Dani laughed and threw her arms around him, tumbling him onto his back on the stage. "There's no one else I'd want to share that with," she said.

Then she threw one leg over his waist, straddling him, and proceeded to show him just how much they both had to look forward to.

About the Author

Kate Davies first tried her hand at romance at the young age of twelve. Sadly, that original science fiction/love story is lost to the ages. But after many years meandering through such varied writing fields as short fantasy fiction, playwriting, poetry, and nonfiction, she's made her way home to romance.

Kate lives in the Pacific Northwest with her husband and kids. When not chasing the rugrats around the house, she loves to write sexy stories about strong, passionate men and women.

Learn more about Kate at www.kate-davies.com, or check out her blog at www.kate-davies.blogspot.com. Join her newsletter group at http://groups.yahoo.com/group/katedaviesupdates/ to keep up to date with new releases, signings, and other news. She can be contacted at kate@kate-davies.com.

Look for these titles

Now Available

Beginnings: Ritual Love

Darcy and Mac are "best friends with benefits", but now Mac wants more than just the hot sex. He wants Darcy forever. And he'll risk everything to get her.

The Boy Next Door
© *2007 Jessica Jarman*

The last thing Darcy Phillips wants after the end of a disastrous relationship is to get involved with another man. Being free and unattached was the plan until her old pal Thomas "Mac" MacAllister strolls back into her life.

Mac has always loved Darcy but the timing was always wrong. Now, she's home and unattached. And after a night of wine and conversation, things turn hot fast. But Darcy isn't ready for more than the physical and she definitely doesn't want anyone knowing what the two of them are up to. Especially her mother.

It isn't long, though, before Mac wants more. Much more. Yet Darcy isn't sure she's willing to risk their long-time relationship for something as dangerous as love. But Mac is a man who knows what he wants and he's not afraid to go after it.

Using their incendiary passion as a starting point, Mac sets out to win the girl of his dreams and show her that everything she wants…is right next door.

Available now in ebook from Samhain Publishing.

When two friends share a night of unbridled passion, can their relationship withstand the consequences?

The Rebound Guy
© *2007 Jennifer Colgan*

Catching her boyfriend in the act with another woman should have made Lauren James angry, indignant or even depressed. Instead, it made her horny. The only man in the world she trusts enough to help her through the sting of betrayal is her best friend, Eric Reynolds.

When Lauren shows up at Eric's apartment, it doesn't take much for her to seduce him. She finds solace for her trampled heart and bruised ego in Eric's capable hands. After an unforgettable night of passion, Lauren wakes to the cold reality that she used Eric to get revenge. Will Eric forgive her, even if she can't forgive herself?

Available now in ebook from Samhain Publishing.

Discover Samhain!
THE HOTTEST NEW PUBLISHER ON THE PLANET

Romance, fantasy, mystery, thriller, mainstream and more—Samhain has more selection, hotter authors, and everything's available in both ebook and print.

Pick your favorite, sit back, and enjoy the ride!
Hot stuff indeed.

WWW.SAMHAINPUBLISHING.COM

GET IT NOW

MyBookStoreAndMore.com

GREAT EBOOKS, GREAT DEALS... AND MORE!

Don't wait to run to the bookstore down the street, or waste time shopping online at one of the "big boys." Now, all your favorite Samhain authors are all in one place—at MyBookStoreAndMore.com. Stop by today and discover great deals on Samhain—and a whole lot more!

WWW.SAMHAINPUBLISHING.COM

Discover eBooks!
THE FASTEST WAY TO GET THE HOTTEST NAMES

Get your favorite authors on your favorite reader, long before they're out in print! Ebooks from Samhain go wherever you go, and work with whatever you carry—Palm, PDF, Mobi, and more.

WWW.SAMHAINPUBLISHING.COM